I0746746

The Way I See It

Series by LB Tillit

Ozzie-Book 1

Ozzie

L.B. Tillit

ISBN: 978-1-7352642-1-9
Published in the United States of America

Dedication

To all who dare to scream loud enough to be heard. And to those who are willing to listen and take action!

Chapter 1

Practice

"Get up and do it again!" Vic screamed. "If you're not throwing up then you are NOT done!"

"Shut up, Vic!" I couldn't help it. The sun was too hot and we had been running the same play for two hours. "I'm getting some water." I didn't really care if Vic was the assistant football coach or not. He wasn't about to kill us before we got to play our first game of the season.

"Ozzie! GET BACK IN LINE!" Vic's voice boomed. I turned to face the assistant coach, a very large man, with arms the size of melons and thighs stretching his shorts to their limits. His hair was cut short and his large hands were wiping the sweat that was pouring off his face. Sometimes it was scary how much he looked like me.

"No." I turned away and walked toward the water. Used paper cups were tossed everywhere, so I went right for one of the large orange water coolers. I pushed the button as I tucked my mouth under the cool stream of water. I tried to drown out Vic's voice yelling at me. I turned slowly to let the water spill all over my head and trickle down my back. When I had finally had enough, I stood up and looked at Vic. I knew he was really pissed because he stopped yelling. He stared at me and his top lip curled up. Like a snarl, but with no sound.

"Hey, Coach?" Someone yelled from the huddle of players still in line. "You think we could get a water break too?"

Vic's eyes never left mine as he yelled. "Ten-minute water break." Half the team quickly made their way to the coolers, while the other half grabbed their own bottles off the benches on the sidelines.

"What the hell was that?" Vic's face moved in close. But still, he had to look up at me. *Look up*. He hated that. I was actually bigger than he was.

I looked down on Vic and shook my head. "You really think we will play better for you when you act like a jackass?" I spit on the ground before I looked at him again. "A real winning move! You think the team will show you respect?"

"They won't with you up in my face!" Vic was the one to move in closer. I glanced over at Coach McCoy who was plopped on a golf cart, the only shade around. He was already as red as a lobster and his shirt was soaked. Some shade was a good idea. With one hand on his belly, he flipped open his own small cooler and pulled out a cold Gatorade.

He took a long, drawn-out gulp, but his eyes never left the scene playing out a few yards away.

Coach McCoy was going to stay out of this. So I looked back down at Vic. He was still waiting for me to respond. "Well," I smiled. "What are brothers for?"

Chapter 2

The Axman

"Your brother is so pissed!" Gavin handed me my helmet as we walked back out onto the field. He pulled his own helmet over his light brown hair that was plastered to his head. His cheeks were bright red. Gavin Sullivan was our quarterback, and as a senior, he was also our captain. Since I was a junior, everyone was betting that next year I'd be made captain of the team.

"He'll get over it," I said as I pulled my helmet on and got myself set up on the line. I tried to sound tough. It seemed to be working since everyone believed I was tough. If I let them know that I doubted every word that came out of mouth, or every movement I made on the field, it would be the end of me. So I made sure that everyone believed that being left tackle was what I lived for. Everyone bought it. And everyone counted on it. It seemed there wasn't a game that didn't leave me wanting more since I could take down two or three linemen at once. I played both defensive and offensive tackle and I always played most of the game. That had been the case for my freshman and sophomore years as well.

I had already outdone my brother's legacy at Hancock High. The Waxman family had raised two generations of football stars. My dad, Mo Waxman, was a Hancock Thunder All-State MVP two years in a row. My brother, Vic, was also a Waxman football star. He wore the Hancock Thunder black and white colors proudly. He was the most-respected "Waxman Legend" until he graduated. That only lasted until that same fall when I hit high school. Even as a freshman, the Waxman magic had shifted to me.

Vic joined Dad and Uncle Jay's moving company three years ago. Waxman and Sons' Movers was well-respected in Midway County. And they had been since Grandpa first started it thirty years ago. Dad and Uncle Jay took it over when Grandpa died. They worked hard to keep the quality at Grandpa's standard. So, since the demand was still great, working for Dad made more sense than following a football career. At least that's what they told me. But Vic's love for football still dominated, so Hancock High was happy to have him help coach. White lightning bolts waving on black flags still lined our driveway. Hancock Thunder ran in our blood.

The whistle blew and Vic had us run the same play he had been drilling into us all afternoon. This time I felt my muscles react without thinking. I moved so swiftly that I took down the defensive lineman and blocked two other players from reaching our star running back, Carlos. Carlos held the ball like a baby as he crossed into the end zone. Everyone was yelling and slapping each other. The familiar chant began to grow. "Axman! Axman! Axman!"

A slap hit my shoulder hard. "That will show your brother!" Gavin yelled. "Good thing the Axman is on our team. Hemby won't know what hit them next week!" Hemby's team, the Hemby Hawks, were our greatest rivals, and every year the season kicked off with all of Hancock showing up. Team rivalry was the glue that held us together.

I replayed what had just happened in my head. How the move had been flawless. How the team had reacted as one. I turned to look at the assistant coach standing on the sidelines. Vic and Coach McCoy were nodding their heads at each other. They were satisfied. We had finally understood what Vic was trying to teach us. He saw me looking at him and he smiled. He knew what he was doing. He had me and the team right where he wanted us.

Chapter 3

Hall

"What is your problem, Ozzie?" Vic's voice came up behind me as I sat on the only good plastic chair on our back patio. It was more like a slab of concrete that had once been cared for, but neglect was beginning to show. Ma was busy working as a large-scale event planner and was gone for days at a time, and Dad was too tired to care. I was wearing my favorite Browns cap. The orange and white stitching stood out on the brown cotton fabric. It was well worn. Dad had given it to me when I was eight as he explained to me that they had named me after Ozzie Newsome Jr., the NFL Hall of Fame tight end that had played for the Cleveland Browns. A real football hero. I felt so proud the day he gave the cap to me. Even if it was too big at the time, over the years my head had grown into it, but I never felt I had grown enough to earn the honor of my namesake. I wore the cap all the time. It reminded me of who I needed to be. I had a long way to go.

I turned and faced my brother. "I don't see why you act like you do at practice and then show up at home and pretend it's all good."

Vic's eyes dropped and he walked up next to me. "Look Ozzie, I know you hate me for it now, but when the scouts see you play like today, you'll have every college ready to give you a full ride." We both looked out across our sorry yard. "Then you can leave *all this* behind." I found it strange that Vic talked about leaving when he still lived at home with us. He didn't seem in any hurry to leave anything behind.

I shook my head. "What if I don't want to?"

Vic looked at me. He frowned and then he slapped my shoulder and laughed. "Funny! Real funny!"

I shook my head at my brother. He didn't get it. I liked football. Lived for the perfect tackle. Soaked up the roar of the crowd. But Vic *loved* football. Dad *loved* football. I kept waiting for that same intensity. I kept pushing myself, showing everyone that I was *made* for football and hoped that one day I would believe it too. Maybe if I tried hard enough, I would feel that *love* for football. Maybe. I forced a smile. "Yeah, just kidding."

"Don't scare me like that, Ozzie!" He turned and went back inside as I stared at the yard again. Vic and I used to throw a football every day after school, with Dad coaching us. The grass was always perfectly mowed, all the way up to the edge of the church property. I could still hear Mom yelling *don't you boys go messing up any graves. Can't have all of Hall jumping down my throat.* Hall Drive, Hall Circle, and Hall Grocery were all part of my neighborhood, which was basically called *Hall.* It had, at one time, been the black neighborhood. A time my parents spoke of often when I was a kid. Mom would talk about old Mrs. Wilkes bringing the best peach cobbler to church potlucks. Zion Baptist was the last sign that Hall was once an active black community. The almost all-black church still stood on River View Drive, proudly overlooking the Rayo River. The small cemetery was the only thing between our house and the church. Zion Baptist used to be packed on Sundays.

But once half of Hall was torn down and the Riverside Apartments built, we lost half our neighbors. Some bought or rented homes in the new suburbs on the north side of town near Delgado Outdoor Mall. Not a bad move. But others had to move west, along Hill View Avenue. The name made it sound great, but it only described the fact that you could see most of the city of Hancock from the windows of the public housing. The apartment buildings lined the ridge, with the I-238 Beltway tucked behind them. In any case, Zion Baptist and Hall were only a memory to most.

"Ozzie?" a voice yelled. I scanned the yard but didn't see anyone. "Over here!" A hand was waving as a head popped out from behind one of the gravestones.

"Vashon?" I stood up and started walking across my yard. It needed mowing. Bad. But I knew I couldn't mow as well as Dad. So I didn't even try, even when he kept yelling at me to do it. I figured he would eventually get to it. "What are you doing sneaking around?"

"I'm not sneaking around!" Vashon frowned. He was lanky and was wearing shorts that stopped right above his knees, revealing chunks of mud caked to his skin. He saw me look at the mud and he quickly brushed it off. "Granny made me come clean up some of the graves."

Mrs. Wilkes had a way to discipline her four grandchildren and I tried not to laugh at the pitiful look on Vashon's face. But I couldn't help myself. "What did you do now?"

"Nothing!" Vashon shifted awkwardly. I moved in closer and towered over the poor boy. I remembered when Ma would promise to watch the Wilkes kids after church, which meant Vic and I had to babysit the brats. Vashon was the oldest.

"Don't lie to me! Are you like twelve now? You shouldn't be lying!" I teased him.

Vashon tried to make himself bigger than he was and crossed his arms over his chest. "I'm fourteen!"

"Could have fooled me!"

"Shut up, man! I'm a freshman this year at your school. Not that you would care!" He turned to walk away from me.

"What? You did not just tell me to shut up!" I started to walk behind the boy as he was walking away. I wasn't really very pissed, but he didn't know that.

He suddenly turned around and faced me. "Okay, man. Back off." I stopped and stared down at him. "Granny wasn't too happy when I borrowed her car." I raised my eyebrows, but he continued. "Just wanted to go to the new movie theater up at the Delgado Mall."

My mouth dropped. "So you stole her car to go see a movie?"

He dropped his arms. Defeated. "I didn't steal the car. I borrowed it." He looked at me and gave me a sneaky smile. Vashon's smile could always make you forgive him for anything.

I tried not to laugh. "Well, you're lucky you are only cleaning up the graveyard and not being buried here."

Vashon shook his head, losing his smile. "You don't get it, man. There is nothing to do here in Hall. I had to get away."

I nodded trying to show him I understood. But I didn't, not really. Vashon knelt down beside a grave and began pulling some weeds. He was done talking and, clearly, I had nothing else to say.

Chapter 4

Zonta

The summer heat did not let up on the first day of school. But summer sure felt like it was over the minute first bell rang. It was more like a loud high-pitched scream.

"Hi, Ozzie." The most beautiful girl at Hancock High came up beside me. Her deep brown eyes looked right into mine. Her wide smile showed every perfectly straight and perfectly white tooth. She was so close to me that her shoulder brushed my arm.

I smiled down at her. "Hi, Zonta. Did you have a good summer?"

"Sure did." She knocked into my arm again, like we were old friends. "I just got back from a weekend in New York City." She looked up at me, still grinning. "How about you?"

I was trying to be nice. She was beautiful. But New York City? Who from Hancock would spend a weekend in New York City? Should I tell her I spent most of my summer prepping for the football season? That my family hadn't gone on a trip since I was ten. And that trip was only two hours away to the Hemby Mountains. It was supposed to be all four of us for a week. Hemby Dude Ranch was going to teach us all about being cowboys. Dad went on and on about how black cowboys helped shape the west, and we ought to be proud to learn all about it. But Mom had to suddenly leave for work and Dad was left with Vic and me. We did have fun. But that was all I knew about family vacations. I sure didn't know anything about quick weekends away. But I didn't want to tell her any of that. So I did what I did best. I didn't answer.

Instead, I smiled and asked, "How was New York?" Her eyes lit up. I took a deep breath. Clearly, she had a lot to say. But I really wasn't in the mood. So before she could answer, I said, "I'm sure you have a lot to talk about, but I don't want to be late for my first class." I lifted up my class schedule. "Looks like I have Ms. Williams for first period."

Zonta's eyes grew wide with excitement. "Me too! U.S. History. Right?"

I held my fake smile as I looked at my paper and then back at her. "Yes. Isn't that something."

"That's great! We can walk together." Zonta quickly looped her honey-brown arm through my arm as she led me to the open door only a few feet away.

I guess I could have pulled away. But I didn't want to be rude. As we walked into the room, I realized I should not have let Zonta pull me into her game so quickly. Every eye was on us. Trying to ignore the stares, I took off my Browns cap and tucked it into my back pack.

"Didn't know you two were sweet on each other!" Carlos yelled across the room. He was wearing his practice jersey from yesterday. He clearly hadn't washed it since he liked to show off the grass stains as if they were badges of honor. I shook my head, but before I could say anything, Blake Dockins, a very pale blond boy that drove me crazy, jumped up and moved in close.

"Oh, yeah! Got you a fine catch, Ozzie." Blake's voice just made me cringe. He was trying way too hard. He tried too hard on the team too, and still sat on the bench most of the time. I was always happy when Coach benched him. It meant I didn't have to listen to him more than I had to. But suddenly he was in class with me as well. Great. I looked at Zonta whose smile quickly faded as she let go of my arm. A few of her giggly girlfriends waved for her to join them. She did.

"Shut up, Blake!" I said as I shoved him back.

"What? What did I do?" Blake clearly had no clue.

"Just shut up, Blake!" Carlos jumped in. He waved at me to sit next to him. But his nasty jersey made me shake my head and just plop down in the closest chair that was not attached to a desk. I couldn't fit in those chair-desks anymore. I slung my backpack onto the small table in front of me. "Whatever!" Carlos was pissed. I didn't care.

I looked across the room at Zonta. She wasn't talking to the girls anymore. I was surprised that she was looking out the window, clearly trying to avoid any more attention. But all you could see was the construction site behind the school. New buildings were replacing an old neighborhood. I wondered whose neighborhood.

I didn't look at any other classmates. I didn't care who else was in the class. I had only been at school ten minutes and I was already over it.

Chapter 5

Hancock High

Ms. Williams walked into the classroom and everyone shut up. She was what most people would call a tall-strong-beautiful-black-woman-you-didn't-mess-with. But really, none of us messed with her because she knew all our parents. Well, at least mine. She'd gone to school with Dad and had graduated from Hancock High. Word was that she went to some fancy college, worked in Washington, D.C., for a time, and then decided to become a teacher and move back home. I remembered Mom and Dad going on about how sad it was for her to return when she could have made something of herself. From where I sat, she didn't look like a loser.

"Why should you care about history?" Ms. Williams' first words made us all look around at each other. Who started a class . . . no . . . a school year, this way?

"Don't you need to take roll?" Blake yelled from the back of the room.

Ms. Williams moved toward the back of the room where Blake and Carlos were sitting. She stopped, crossed her arms, and gave him a look. One of those that took in *all* of Blake. She started at the top of his blond head and then slowly scanned her eyes over him until she was inspecting his first-day-of-school shoes. Nikes, of course. Then scanned her way back up over his American Eagle jeans, with the perfectly placed holes. By the time she met his crystal blue eyes she finally spoke. "Blake Dockins."

"Yes, ma'am!"

She then looked at the boy in front of him. "Mateo Meza-Moya."

A stocky Hispanic boy, with his long black hair pulled back in a ponytail, barely looked up from his notebook where he was writing something. "Here." White earbuds had been tossed to the edge of his desk. Mateo always wore them when he wasn't in class. It seemed they were *always* within reach or in his ears.

Ms. Williams continued, pointing at an Asian girl on the other side of the room, who looked like she was pissed at something. "Emma Tang-Lee." The girl nodded without answering. Our teacher moved through the classroom saying everyone's name. She finally reached the far window. "Zonta Jones." Zonta didn't say anything at first, still looking out the window. Ms. Williams raised her voice, "Zonta Jones?"

Zonta quickly turned her head, pulled earbuds from her ears. "So sorry." Her bright eyes and huge smile returned. As sweet as ever. "I didn't know class had started."

The class broke into laughter. Zonta frowned and quickly tucked away her earbuds and phone. Ms. Williams did not raise her voice, but responded. "Miss Jones. Class starts when you walk into the room." Zonta nodded and kept her eyes on the teacher as the class settled.

But Ms. Williams was not finished. "Blake Dockins?" Blake's shoulders dropped. He wouldn't look her in the eyes. I thought he deserved whatever was coming. "If I were you, I would assume from now on that I have already taken roll the minute I walk into the room. Should I continue?" Several of the students who had not been called yet, looked at Ms. Williams waiting for her to call on them.

"Yes, ma'am . . . I mean, no, ma'am." Blake tried to answer but gave up finding the right words. Instead, as soon as Ms. Williams turned away, he sat back in his chair with relief.

"So I ask again. Why should you care about history?" Ms. Williams moved to the front of the class and perched on top of a tall stool. She waited. And waited. And waited. I thought, for a minute, we would all fail this class if someone didn't answer soon.

Finally, Emma Tang-Lee raised her hand and rolled her eyes as she answered, ". . . so we don't repeat it."

"Well, Miss Tang-Lee, it seems you have stated the most over-used statement about history that there is. *And* you rolled your eyes." Ms. Williams paused. "It seems either you think the answer is too easy, or you don't believe it."

"Both." Emma quickly answered.

"Explain." Ms. Williams was not letting it go.

Emma sat up in her seat, more bothered than anything. "Well, we clearly cannot repeat history. It is *never* the same. People may still do the same stupid things again and again. But it's *never* the same history. It's always new. New ways to hate. New ways to oppress, new ways to fight wars. But never the same."

Ms. Williams raised her eyebrows. "So, always bad then. History is always bad?"

"Well, pretty much." Emma sighed.

"But what about the great things? Like new buildings?" Zonta pointed out the construction outside the window.

"Or the newest video game." Carlos winked at Zonta. She did not smile back. Several students giggled, causing Zonta to shift awkwardly. I wanted to say something, but I did not want any of the attention. So I settled for trying to smile at Zonta, but she wasn't looking my way.

"Okay, good." Ms. Williams stood up and paced. "So, clearly we all have different takes on history." She turned to face us again. "So I ask once more. Why should you *care* about history?"

"Because it tells us who we are today." A voice from the hall answered. Ms. Williams turned quickly to see who had spoken. A girl appeared. She was white, with a sunburn blistering on her forehead. Her greasy dirty-blond hair was long and hanging in her face. She might have been a little on the chubby side, but you couldn't quite tell because her clothes were way too big. She wore sweats that dragged the floor, with toes and old flip-flops peeking through. A pink T-shirt hung on her. At second glance, I realized it may have been red at one time. She awkwardly shifted the camo-green backpack on her shoulder.

Ms. Williams smiled and waved her in. "I knew I was missing one. You must be Lilly Orem. Welcome to Hancock High."

Chapter 6

Lunch

Lunch couldn't come fast enough. History seemed to drag on as soon as the teacher got the new girl to sit down in the far back corner and the rest of the class to stop staring at her. I stopped the minute she walked by me. I hated it when people stared. I wasn't about to be one of those people. Ms. Williams went on about how the new girl's answer was one worth talking about, but maybe later. I knew that meant she was ready to move on. She needed to hand out her notes on what to expect that year. As she began to go over the list, I tuned her out.

Second-period English class was easy enough. I was grateful Zonta and most of my first period were not in my class. The drama was too much. But the new girl walked in late, again. I didn't think much of it and was happy when the lunch bell finally rang.

The cafeteria was on the ground floor of Hancock High. A huge window covered an entire wall, lighting up the tables that spread across a freshly waxed floor. Some students grabbed their lunches and headed through double doors to the outside patio and lawn. It wasn't more than a slab of concrete that had a few metal tables with benches attached, each bolted down. The "lawn" was mostly dead grass, at least for a while. It spread out toward trailers that held some add-on classrooms. The trailers messed up what used to be the best place to hang out during lunch.

I grabbed two helpings of mashed potatoes, two burgers, a pile of banana pudding, two protein bars, and four milks. I sat down inside with Gavin. As quarterback, he would talk about Friday's game and I could just listen. He liked to think he knew it all, and that was okay with me. I needed to eat. I really needed to gain weight. I was 6'4" and a strong 270 lbs., but Vic said that I'd really be noticed at 290 lbs.

Carlos and Blake sat down across the table and joined Gavin to discuss the plays. I nodded once in a while. That was enough. They thought I cared. I didn't. I knew I was good, and I knew I could follow any play we'd learned. Talking about it, though, helped them remember what to do. So I figured it was good for them to replay what worked and what didn't.

It wasn't long before they moved from football to trashing people. They threw out comments all the time full of hateful stereotyping. They didn't hold back. Race, gender, or any trait at all were fair game.

That day was no different than all the rest. Blake pointed out some new Hispanic girls walking by and said, "Look, more Mexicans!"

Carlos and Gavin laughed as Carlos added, "More tacos for me!" He air-kissed the girls' backs as they kept walking. He added, "Better than eating Chinese egg rolls!" He pointed two tables over at Emma, from first period, who was sitting with her friends, minding her own business. "Right, Ozzie?"

I looked at Carlos and frowned. "What?"

"You wouldn't eat any egg rolls, would you?" He pointed at Emma, still in her own world. Nobody could hear the trash talk, so I usually didn't care and faded in and out of listening. But this time he asked me a direct question. I decided to play dumb and pretend he wasn't making a racist comment. "I eat egg rolls all the time!" Carlos, Gavin and Blake all broke out in laughter. I frowned again and brushed them off as they laughed at me. It was easier to be laughed at than to stand up to their racist and sexist comments.

Carlos checked out three more girls that walked by. Two black and one white. He licked his lips and soaked up every curve and sway. "I like all sorts of flavors and sizes."

Suddenly they grew quiet. I looked up from my food. "What?" They were looking behind me, so I turned. They were all watching Zonta walk by.

"Damn!" Gavin said. "She sure filled out this summer."

Carlos blew a low whistle. Zonta looked for a second at Carlos and turned her head away. She wasn't too happy. "Yes! And in all the right places! She's a creamy caramel, ready to melt in my mouth."

"Shut up, man!" I said it before I knew it. I told myself I'd stay out of this. I wasn't sure why I said anything. So I tried to blow it off and act tough. "Getting a little tired of all this talk of food. Can't you be a little more *exact* when you talk about people?"

"Come on, Ozzie!" Carlos faked a whine. He quickly grinned. "I'll give you *exact*. Don't you think she's fine and hot as hell and want to...?"

"I said shut up!" I shook my head. I never bothered to stand up to Carlos before. Why at that moment? And was I really standing up to him? I had to think quickly to keep my tough image alive. "Looks like you can't handle a pretty girl when you see one. You might think about trying to talk *to* them and not dish out trash *about* them. At your rate you will never get to taste ANY fruit!" Blake and Gavin laughed as Carlos took the dig. He clutched his chest and acted like he was deeply wounded.

Gavin smiled. "Oh, I get it!"

"Get what?" I frowned. Then I looked at Zonta. She had heard me. She nodded at me and smiled before she turned to head outside.

Chapter 7

Friday Night Football

I managed to get through the rest of the week avoiding eye contact with Zonta and not talking to anyone, except at practices. It seemed to work. Mind my own business and everyone would leave me alone.

"You ready?" Vic came up behind me as I was squeezing the black jersey over my shoulder pads. He helped me shove the last of the plastic armor into place. The number 55 stood out in bold white across my back. One day, if I did everything right, WAXMAN would be added to the back of a professional football jersey.

"Always." I answered. It was what I said. It was what he expected. It was what Coach McCoy expected. It was what the team expected.

Vic slapped my shoulders. "That's right! You are!" He turned to the rest of the team in the locker room and Coach McCoy.

"Alright, boys." Coach McCoy demanded our attention. "It starts now." We all faced the heavyset man. Even though Vic could still run plays with us, Coach McCoy was the man we all respected. All listened to. "The Hemby Hawks won't know what hit them! *They* will walk away tonight defeated. *You* will walk away winners. *You* will claim tonight as a your own. Hancock Thunder *will* dominate."

The team began to nod and grunt, "Yeah!"

Coach McCoy wasn't finished. "Offensive line! Don't let them get to Sullivan." He pointed at Gavin. Our fearless quarterback and captain had to be protected. Although Gavin was almost as tall as I was, he was not quite 200 lbs. Anyone my size might do some real damage if they tackled him. Coach continued, "Own the line of scrimmage and we will own the game!" He looked at me.

The team started to chant, "Axman, Axman, Axman." I smiled and nodded my thanks and could see Vic grinning. He was proud. I suddenly felt proud too.

Coach McCoy was right. We were ruthless. It felt like we were suddenly in the playoffs, not the first game of the season. I listened to Gavin call the plays and didn't miss a step. No one touched our quarterback.

At halftime we were winning, 28 to 3. Carlos and Hunter Burns were our best running backs and Hunter had been taken down hard, twice. But it was really nothing compared to the hits we delivered to the Hemby Hawks. Some were limping off the field. Still, Hunter was pissed. Owen, a lineman like me, had been beaten twice on a couple of plays, and Hunter got nailed hard by the Hemby defense. Carlos had been getting nice yards since he was running the left side. My side. No Hemby player got a clean shot at him. I was covered in dirt and sweat and I knew I would need to soak in ice once it was over. "Why can't Ozzie move to the right side for once?" Hunter was up in Vic's face. He would never dare complain to Coach McCoy.

"You were only hit twice you pissant!" Owen walked up to Hunter. His heavily freckled face and flaming red hair made him look like he was on fire. He was covered in dirt and sweat. "I got beat twice. So what? Maybe you should run faster and put a little more shoulder into them. Wait. Are you afraid of getting hurt?" Owen was big, but not as big as me. Yet, his stocky size and quick footing meant he could tackle someone, go down hard and then jump back up on his feet without missing a beat. Hunter's dark skin seemed even darker with Owen's freckled face almost touching the running back's scowling face. I thought I heard Hunter begin to growl.

"Wait a minute!" Carlos walked up. He didn't want to miss the action. His shirt had a few grass stains on it from his three touchdowns, including two dramatic diving catches in the endzone. "Don't want to lose the magic do you, Coach Vic?"

"Could use a little Axman magic myself!" Hunter wasn't joking and glared at Owen. "Had enough of Hemby!"

Owen fumed. His last name was Hemby. He knew Hunter wasn't talking about the other team. He couldn't help that his last name was Hemby. Almost every neighborhood had a Hemby. The family went way back. The Hemby River that emptied into Midway Lake and the Hemby Mountains to the west reminded us that certain families made their mark years ago. It didn't help Owen any, though. He lived in Hancock.

"Sounds like a good idea!" Vic said as he looked between Owen and Hunter. I was furious. Since when did a player get Vic to change his plays?

Owen flung his helmet at his locker. "That's a bunch of bull!"

Vic went up to Owen and got up in his face. "You think I would have listened to Hunter if you hadn't shown your ass just now? I don't trust you'll get out there and block for him in the second half." I was standing, shaking my head, hoping Owen would convince Vic that he *would* block for Hunter, even if he was pissed.

But Owen just ran his freckled hand through his red hair, leaving a steak of dirt. "Whatever!"

Vic stared at him a minute longer and then walked toward me. But before he could say anything, I whispered, "But we didn't run any offensive plays with me on the right!" I didn't have the plays in my head. We hadn't run them. I hadn't learned them. I felt my heart race.

"So?" Vic slapped my shoulder. "You got to be able to be moved around. Just like you do on defense."

"Then you should have had me practice it!" I glared. But my fear was not easily masked.

"And have you miss those perfect plays in the first half?" Vic grinned.

"But they were perfect because we were ready!" I practically growled. I looked at the rest of them who were avoiding Owen and waiting for Coach McCoy to come into the locker room. Coach liked to take his time. Shake a few hands, slap a few backs. Fall Friday nights were his. He loved the attention.

"You got this, Ozzie!" Vic meant it. He believed I could switch from the left side of the line to the right side. Like it was nothing! He believed I was that good. He looked at my face and frowned. "What's wrong?" When I didn't answer he added. "You've played football since you could walk! You've played pickup games a thousand times! You know everything there is to know about football. You've even played quarterback in our back yard. What's your problem?"

"This game was perfectly planned. This is *not* part of the plan." It made perfect sense to me. So I really didn't understand when he walked away shaking his head, muttering something under his breath.

Coach McCoy showed up with only a few minutes of half time left. The marching band was blasting their final notes as the crowd cheered. Coach began to speak, but I didn't hear a word he said. I dropped my head and stared at the white lightning bolts painted onto the side of my black helmet. My brother didn't understand what he was asking me to do. I understood how to be *perfect* with *perfect* pre-planned plays. For me, *winging it* was impossible.

Chapter 8

Winging It

It was only a few minutes into the second half when I noticed the change. The cheering was not as loud. At least it seemed that way. I focused hard on what I was doing. But it was like being left-handed after being right-handed my whole life. On our first offensive series my blocks turned the Hemby lineman right into our running backs. So we had to punt. Hunter grumbled something I couldn't hear. But Gavin told me to shake it off and that we'd get the ball back. He was right. We held Hemby to no gain, so they had to punt. With the ball back in Gavin's hands, I was dead set to make it right. I would hold the line so our running backs could make their plays. Coach's play call was for a reverse, with Hunter carrying the ball. Problem was that I became reversed and plowed right into Hunter, just as he got the handoff. I knocked the ball right out of the crook of his arm. A white jersey with red letters grabbed it and ran. The Hemby Hawks made their first touchdown. After their kicker secured the extra point, we were suddenly 28 to 10.

The silence was quickly filled with roars from the visitors that were crammed into the old wooden bleachers across the field from the new concrete home bleachers. The home crowd, wearing black and white, rose with the concrete well above the visitors' side. As the visitors cheered, red flags waving, a slow and steady booing began to rise out of the sea of black and white.

The whistle blew and Coach McCoy called a time-out. I felt the sweat burn my eyes as I reached the sidelines. Coach grabbed my helmet and pulled me in to his face. His voice rose above the cheerleaders and band lifting a fight song. "What the hell was that?" His voice was not so much angry as confused.

"Sorry, Coach," was all I could say. I let one of the middle-school football players, who acted as our water-boys, shoot cool water into my mouth and all over my face.

"Got to be the heat, Coach," Gavin yelled as he moved in next to me and soaked up his share of cool water.

The coach looked at the quarterback. "Sullivan, if I want your input, I will ask for it!" He pointed at the other players who were waiting for direction from the time-out huddle. "Go and act like a quarterback and call a play that will keep us in the lead." Gavin nodded and returned to the huddle. As I moved to join him, coach grabbed the back of my shoulder pad. "Not you *Axman*! Take a seat!" Coach then yelled, "Dockins! Get in there!" Blake's eyes went wide as he looked at me, then at Coach and then at the ground. He swallowed and quickly shoved his bite guard into his mouth as he ran onto the field. He looked almost half my size. Coach looked at me one last time and growled, "I *said,* take a seat!"

I hesitated a minute, but Coach's red face and scowl made it clear he was not joking. So I finally walked off the field and over to the benches. I saw Vic standing with his arms crossed. He didn't look at me. Not once. I had never been benched. Not for messing up. But the thing was, I didn't feel embarrassed. I felt anger. How dare Vic switch up my position! How dare he make me do what I hadn't practiced!

Still, the team won the game without me. But just by 3 points.

Chapter 9
Lilly

11:03pm filled my phone's screen as I took it out of my pocket to check the bus schedule. I had just left the locker room wearing my Browns cap low over my face, hoping no one would see me. But when I saw how dark it was and found the parking lot empty, I shoved it back out of my face. My plan had worked. I had waited for everyone to leave. I didn't want to hear anyone tell me to shake it off or give me a play-by-play on what happened. Or, even worse: feel sorry for me. I knew Vic and Dad had left and I would have to catch the bus. But I didn't care. A little longer without them tearing into me would be worth the bus ride. I had enough time to catch the 11:20 bus at the corner of 17th Street and Seaberg Avenue.

It was muggy and I was already sweating again as I slung my duffle bag over my shoulder and stepped onto the sidewalk. "What happened?" A voice came up behind me. I jumped back against the chain-link fence that followed the sidewalk. I was ticked at myself for looking at the phone instead of the street. I found myself looking down at a wide-eyed white girl. T-shirt, sweatpants and flip-flops. It was the new girl, Lilly. "Sorry I scared you." She took a step back. She dropped her camo-green backpack on the sidewalk in front of her. She reached into a side pocket and pulled out a water bottle. She drank deeply and then offered the rest up to me.

I shook my head, trying not to show my disgust, and moved away from the fence. "You didn't scare me!"

Lilly looked up at me. I was shocked when the street light lit up her bright green eyes. I had never seen eyes so green before. I stared a second too long because suddenly she smiled. "If you say so." She finished the water, tucked the empty bottle back into her bag, and stood back up. The flickering street lights also drew attention to the shine on her face. She grabbed the edge of her T-shirt and pulled it up to wipe off the sweat off her forehead. Her very white underbelly peaked out for a second before the T-shirt dropped back over it. The shirt hung lopsided and she clearly could care less. I frowned. I wasn't sure what she wanted, so I awkwardly started walking along 17th street. I didn't want to miss my bus. I felt her follow me, at first. Then her dirty-blond head came into view bobbing along side of me. I tried not to look at her, hoping she would go away if I didn't pay her any attention. Like a stray dog.

I took out my phone and checked my feed.

Axman 8 dirt

was Axman blind

check this video out

Five different videos popped up, all from different angles, with my epic fail. I swiped out of the feed and shoved my phone in my back pocket.

A car drove by and beeped. A voice screamed, "GO THUNDER!" and then sped off. Before I reached the bus stop, two more cars passed beeping or raising voices to Hancock's win. Lilly was still there. She stopped too.

"They got over your mess-up quickly, didn't they?" Lilly plopped down on the only bench as I stood in front of the metal pole that marked the exact place to start the line for the bus. Not that we needed to form a line.

"They probably didn't notice." I couldn't believe I had answered her.

Lilly laughed, "Oh, I'm sure they did! If I noticed, then they noticed." I looked at her and frowned as she pointed at herself. "Because I know *nothing* about football. And *even I* saw you take out your own player and lose that ball!"

I felt myself heat up. Who was she to think she could talk to me like this? "What do you want from me?"

Lilly jumped up and walked over to me. She leaned on the metal pole, so I stepped back. There wasn't a line anyway. She smiled. "Well, tell me what happened?"

My eyebrows rose as my mouth dropped. "I don't know you! Why should I tell you what happened?"

She dropped her head for a minute, like she was thinking. She quickly looked back up at me and flung out her hand. "Lilly Orem. Nice to meet you Ozzie Axman."

"Waxman." I corrected her as I shook her hand, which was slightly sticky.

"Oh, that makes sense!" She dropped my hand and did a chopping motion. I shook my head at her and then looked down the dark road, hoping to see bus head lights. When I faced her again, she said, "Well, now that we know each other, tell me!"

I shifted my duffle bag to my other shoulder. "No." I was tired.

"Oh." Lilly's voice was soft, which made me look at her. Really look at her. Even though her sunburned forehead was almost healed, her nose was peeling from a new burn. I let my eyes scan the rest of her, from top to bottom. Her backpack looked heavy, packed with God-knows-what. I couldn't quite tell, but it seemed she was wearing the same faded red shirt. Her sweats were dragging the ground leaving random holes. I quickly looked up at her, frowning. No, disgusted. She noticed my intense observation and reaction. She nodded as she backed herself up to the bench again. As she sat down, Lilly dropped her pack on the bench next to her and added, "I get it. You don't want to see me." She laid down on the bench, her long hair spilling over the side. The strange girl looked up at the dark night sky to spot the few stars that were visible through the haze.

She was quiet and didn't say anything else. I looked for bus lights again. There were none, so I walked over to her. "What does that even mean?" I readjusted the cap on my head.

She didn't sit up and didn't even look at me. "I think you know what it means."

"No, I don't." I was frustrated with her. But I wasn't sure why I should even care. She obviously didn't care about herself enough to change her clothes or wash. Instantly, I felt a need to wash my hands.

She still didn't look at me. "Go on. You don't want to see me *AND* you don't want to be seen. So I won't see you." She covered her eyes with her elbow. "Go on. I'll be alright."

The bus pulled up and I quickly moved to get on. As I started to move to my seat, the bus driver asked me, "Is the girl coming?"

I looked out the window at Lilly who hadn't moved. "No, sir. It doesn't look like it."

As we drove off, I felt relief. She was finally gone. But suddenly my stomach dropped. I had just left a teen girl alone. At a bus stop. In the middle of the night.

Chapter 10

Dad

I pushed Lilly out of my head as I walked into the house. I didn't owe Lilly anything. Hell, I didn't even know her. She was weird and, besides, I had enough issues of my own.

I wasn't surprised to find the light on and Dad sprawled in his favorite recliner. I thought, for sure, it would topple over backwards at any moment. "Dad? You still awake?"

With a sudden jerk, he turned his head and smiled at me. "Yep, sure am. Just fighting off sleep until you came home." I helped him get up out of his chair, even though he was still a strong ox himself. He and Uncle Jay could still handle moving a couch up several flights of stairs as if it was a simple, but heavy, puzzle to solve. I looked down the dark hall toward our bedrooms. He squeezed my arm. "Vic's not here. He's with Tamika." Tamika was Vic's girlfriend. They had been together for two years and he'd crash at her place when he felt like it. I wasn't surprised he was with her instead of here, dealing with me. Dad squeezed my arm again to get my attention. "I told him to lay off you until tomorrow."

I nodded and felt a little relief. "Thanks, Dad."

Standing next to me, Dad was still a giant to me. Even though I looked down at him. Like Vic. They had only ever reached 6'2". But they always felt bigger. Stronger. He smiled and patted my shoulder. "I told Vic that he better think really hard before he puts all the blame on you!"

"But, Dad, I really messed up." It was the first time all night that I had said, or even thought, those words.

"You sure did, son." Dad let his hand rest on my shoulder. "But the coach has always got to take some responsibility. Always." I nodded as he continued. "I told Vic he better look at what he turned you into, and then decide what kind of player he wants you to be."

I let my anger toward Vic begin to simmer again. I knew it was his fault! "Yeah! That's right!" It came out like a whine. I cleared my throat and tried again. "I mean . . . okay . . . thanks, Dad."

Dad sighed and finally headed down the hallway, he turned to face me one last time. "You *did* have a hell of a first half, son. I'm proud of you." I smiled and turned to head into the kitchen. His voice followed me, but he was really talking more to himself than me. "We'll add clips from the first half of the game to the highlight video and send it off to the coaches that are already showing an interest. They will be fighting to sign you!"

As his voice trailed off, I felt that pit in my stomach deepen. I grabbed a bowl, a spoon, whole box of Frosted Flakes and a jug of milk as I headed for my room. I threw my Browns cap on the floor and sat on my bed. Reality was, even with blaming Vic, I still could not answer Lilly's question, because I didn't know. As I poured my cereal, I figured maybe I could plug that pit long enough to figure out how to fix whatever had happened.

Chapter 11

The Good Rumor

"Great game, Ozzie!" Zonta quickly walked up next to me as we headed to class. Saturday and Sunday Vic had left me alone, clearly brooding over what Dad had said. I left him alone too, but still dreaded Monday's practice. We had to speak sooner or later.

"Thanks, I guess." I frowned and then looked at Zonta who was grinning and walking along as if nothing at happened. So I asked, "Did you even go to the game?"

Zonta shook her head, still smiling. "Oh, no, I didn't. Not because I didn't want to, mind you, but we had some family plans . . . Anyway, the rumor is that it was an awesome first half . . ." she reached in, touched my arm, and acted all excited as she explained, ". . . and that the heat got to you, so they got you cooled down, but by then they decided to go easy on Hemby." She leaned in like she had a secret as she whispered, ". . . and save you for this week's away game against

Delgado High." She smiled really big and then took off to go grab a book from her locker.

I had planned to walk down the hall and not look anyone in the eye. Instead, I lifted my head to look at the other students' reactions. Was it just Zonta that believed that lie? A few heads nodded at me like they were in on this "secret." A few other girls giggled and told me what a good job I had done. Even our custodian, Mr. Soza, looked up from mopping up a spilled soda and said, "Heat will take down even the best of us! Good to see you, man." He reached out his one empty hand and fist-bumped me.

By the time I reached U.S. History, I was beginning to believe it myself. Maybe it was heatstroke. Maybe I hadn't hydrated enough. Maybe it wasn't my fault.

"You better?" Blake walked through the door in front of me and, for once, his voice didn't annoy me.

I nodded. "Yeah." I didn't know what else to say.

Blake suddenly smiled. "Good! Because I don't ever want to cover your position again. I about died out there. My head and my body are still messed up. And, see this!" He pulled up his shirt and a huge bruise covered his ribs. Then he proceeded to touch it, causing himself to wince. "Hurts like hell."

"Oh, Blake! Does it hurt?" Chastity Shaw, our head cheerleader came up to him. Her long, wavy brown hair was perfectly braided along one side of her head. Her light green eyes stood out under her heavy makeup that made her face and neck look like two different shades of white. She gently touched the bruise again and watched Blake wince again, but this time he smiled at her. Like she could touch his bruise all she wanted. But then quickly looked away. Was he trying to play shy? I thought I would be sick and headed to my seat, letting their flirting go on without me.

Carlos walked by and did his usual fist bump and trash talk, but nothing else. Zonta made it to class right before the bell rang and winked at me as she headed to her seat. I wondered what had gotten into everyone.

Ms. Williams finally started class and had us turning in our weekend's assignment when the door opened and Lilly walked in. Late. Again. We all looked at her. She looked rough. She had managed to change her shirt, a black one this time with a white Hancock Thunder lightning bolt down the front, but the nasty sweats still hung on her. She'd pulled her messy hair into a loose ponytail, but it was already trying to escape. "You're late, Miss Orem!"

"Yes, ma'am." Lilly walked up to her and handed her the tardy slip before heading to her seat at the back of the room. As she passed me,

I looked up at her. But she didn't stop. She didn't turn her head. She acted like I wasn't even alive.

I shook my head, not because she ignored me. But because I realized she was the only one in the school that was right about me.

Chapter 12

The Fix

"Okay, let's run some new plays. We'll work it out." Vic's first words to me since Friday night's game didn't surprise me. Better to move on. Better to ignore his anger. And much better to pretend he knew how to fix the problem. Me.

I nodded. "I'm ready." I joined the rest of my team to warm up. As we moved through the drills, I watched Coach McCoy talk to my brother. As he laid out his new plan, Vic's arms moved about as fast as his mouth. Coach was listening intensely; his head nodded and he glanced at me a couple of times.

"What do you think they're talking about?" Gavin asked between drills.

I shook my head. "How to make sure I don't *overheat* next game!"

Gavin laughed and slapped my shoulder. "Well, I'll take you *overheating* any day! Better than having Blake get crushed like a bug."

"I heard that!" Blake yelled from the sidelines. He had to sit out the next game and several practices until he healed. Ended up he had a bad concussion along with his bruised ribs. But he still had to show up. He wore dark sunglasses and a ball cap and was slowly walking around picking up discarded equipment. Coach McCoy wasn't going to have him do nothing.

"It's true and you know it!" Gavin yelled back.

I laughed, thankful for the distraction.

It only lasted a minute, though. Vic and Coach McCoy finally headed toward us. Coach didn't look at me as he cleared his throat and announced, "We have some new plays to run." The team groaned at first. But were immediately quiet when coach slammed his clipboard to the ground. "I DON'T WANT TO HEAR ANOTHER SOUND OUT OF ANYONE!" We all waited in silence. Finally, Coach continued, "If we are to make it to the playoffs and have a shot at being state champions this year, then I expect you to act like champions. If you don't care about football and this team, then leave now!" We all began to glance at each other, waiting to see if he was talking to anyone in particular. When no one walked off the field, the team looked back at their coach. "Are you in?"

"YES, SIR!" We all yelled, like soldiers ready to return to battle after a defeat. But we had not been defeated. Not as a team. We had won.

Only I had been defeated. But Vic had convinced the coach to have the whole team take responsibility.

I felt a slow simmer rise within me. It wasn't their fault. It was mine. But I didn't say anything. Instead, I took my guilt and anger and let it feed my fire inside. I told myself I could use this fire to make it up to the team. I didn't need to say anything. I would pull off proving myself to my team, or die trying.

We ran new plays all practice. I was focused and ready. They had me jump from left to right tackle without warning. The worst was when they didn't tell me the play and told me to figure it out. I saw red. But I delivered. Not because I had suddenly learned something new. But because my team did not deserve to be punished because of me. And my weakness.

Coach McCoy and Vic smiled at the end of practice, proud of what they had achieved.

I hoped their "fix" would pay off on Friday's away game.

Chapter 13

Mom

"How was practice?" Mom's voice surprised me as Vic and I walked into the kitchen late Thursday afternoon. The week had flown by with practices pushing us to our limits. But there was excitement about the away game. Vic and I were talking again, but never about last Friday night. It almost felt normal again. And, with Mom home, things always felt better. The smell of spaghetti and meatballs hit me as hard as the sight of my mother grinning at me with her arms wide open.

"Mom!" I felt like a six-year-old hugging my mother. "Didn't think you were coming home until Saturday." Even though I looked down at my mother, Rita Waxman was quite a sizable woman. She was broad and tall and carried herself like a queen. A queen we all believed her to be. Dad told us he married her because she was as strong as he was, but we knew it was because he was lucky enough to catch her eye.

"Tomorrow's wedding was canceled, so I headed on home. Seems the bride had second thoughts." Mom turned her head to find Vic behind her, snatching a meatball. "What, Vic? Meatball more important than hugging your mother?" Vic grinned and popped one more meatball into his mouth before he came in for a hug. This left me to sneak toward the pile of meat already smothered in sauce. "Don't you even think about it, Ozzie!" Mom's voice teased. She turned around with both hands on her hips. "Not until you clean up your filthy self." She looked at her dress with new dirt smudges. "Looks like I may even need to clean up before dinner."

"Mom, we're starving!" Vic fussed.

Mom stood her ground and looked at both of us. "What are you, twelve?"

Vic walked up to Mom and planted a messy kiss on her cheek. "Only when you're here!"

I took that moment to snatch two meatballs of my own. "Ozzie!" Mom grabbed the closest spoon she could find and chased us down the hall. We were two grown men being chased by our mother. And loving every minute.

Chapter 14

Maybe

"Too bad I can't play tonight," Blake said before he bit into his pizza. The lunchroom was buzzing with excitement. Taking on the Delgado Bulldogs was almost as big a deal as the Hemby Hawks.

"Well, we will sure miss you!" Carlos smirked. "NOT!"

"You *know* you will!" Blake teased back, but we all knew there was some truth to Carlos's statement. Blake spent most of his time on the bench anyway, so being "benched" until he healed didn't feel any different than usual. Except for one change that only mattered to me. Since Blake was also off the field during practice drills, I found myself less annoyed with him. In general.

Gavin held up his phone and said, "You got to check out this pic from Chastity!" Carlos grabbed Gavin's phone, and his eyebrows shot up before he passed it to Blake.

Blake looked shocked at first and looked away, but quickly said, "I told you she had some great—"

"Good luck tonight." Zonta's voice shut Blake up. Gavin grabbed his phone and quickly flipped it face down. But Zonta didn't seem to notice, because she was looking at me. She smiled sweetly and then waited awkwardly, not sure if she should keep walking or wait for a response.

My mouth was full of chicken and gravy, so I nodded at her. I tried to smile, but I quickly grabbed my napkin to wipe away the gravy dripping down my chin. Instead of turning away in disgust, Zonta giggled and then moved on.

"Dude!" Gavin pointed in Zonta's direction. "She's so into you!" Blake and Carlos were nodding.

"What?" I looked at Zonta and watched her glance back at me once before sitting with her friends. "For real?"

"*For real* is right." Gavin laughed. Sitting across the table from me, Gavin let gravy run down his chin, smiling like an idiot.

Carlos grabbed a napkin, wiped Gavin's chin, and squeaked, "Ohhhh, Ozzie, let me wipe that for you!"

Gavin played along. "Oh, Zonta, you can wipe my chin any time!"

Carlos added, still pretending to be Zonta. "I know some other places I'd like to wipe down too—"

"Shut up." I said as loudly as I could without drawing more attention. "She'll hear you!"

I glanced toward Zonta who was busy talking to her friends. I was relieved.

"See?" Gavin smiled. "She's got you all shook!"

"No, she doesn't." I looked at the guys who all raised their eyebrows.

Carlos's eyes narrowed. Never a good sign. "So, if you're not sweet on her then I can go and make a move." He stood up. "Maybe she's got some pics to share."

"Wait!" I growled. "Sit down."

Carlos plopped back into his seat. "That's what I thought!"

"Look, Ozzie," Gavin wasn't teasing. "She's hot and she's rich. AND she wants you! What else can you ask for?"

I took a deep breath. They weren't wrong. Zonta was the most beautiful girl I had ever seen. But what really mattered to me was that she was always nice to me. Not fake nice, but really nice. I didn't know what was wrong with me. I had never realized that maybe she was nice because she was *into* me. I suddenly felt myself grin as I looked at the guys and said, "Maybe I'll ask her out."

"No dude," Gavin laughed. "Not *maybe*!"

Chapter 15

Pissed

Right after school, the football team, cheerleaders, and marching band were busy loading the activity buses near the stadium. With all the noise and yelling, I almost didn't see the girl straddling the wall behind me. The wall rose only a few feet and wrapped around one side of the grounds. It was a poor attempt to keep people from sneaking in on game days without paying at the front gate. Lilly had learned, like so many others, that the wall was easy to climb onto and made a perfect place to perch and stare at everything going on. Lilly was clearly taking time to watch the organized chaos as she ate a bag of chips. I hadn't talked to Lilly since last Friday and, honestly, hadn't thought much about her. Except I still remembered how I felt after leaving her at the bus stop. Alone. So, I guess, that bit of guilt made me think I should talk to her. At some point.

Suddenly a head popped up out of nowhere and two dark, lanky arms reached for the top of the wall. In an instant, Vashon Wilkes was sitting next to Lilly and they were both laughing. I had forgotten that Vashon had started high school. It seemed like ages ago that he was cleaning up the graveyard behind our house.

Curious, I straightened my Browns cap and I decided to head toward them. I was halfway there before they noticed me. Lilly slowly frowned when she realized I was heading her way. Her dirty-blond hair looked less greasy and, even though she was still wearing the nasty sweats, she had on a blue T-shirt. Lilly knew I was checking out her clothes, which caused her frown to deepen. Vashon, though, grinned and waved. "Hey, Ozzie."

"What's up, Vashon." I looked at Lilly briefly and then back at the smiling idiot. Didn't he know he should stay away from her? She was a junior *and* she wasn't from here. "You okay, man?"

Lilly suddenly crumpled up her empty chip bag and made a shot at the huge trashcan three feet away, missing it. But she didn't care. "Can we help you?" Lilly's bright green eyes flashed my way for less than a second before she looked back at Vashon. She was pissed.

"Lilly, it's okay. This is my old friend, Ozzie." Vashon waved dramatically between us. "Ozzie, this is Lilly."

"Yeah, we've met." Lilly didn't smile or look at me.

I explained, "We have two classes together."

Vashon nodded like he understood, but the frown on his face began to deepen. Lilly finally faced me and laughed, "Oh, yes! So you noticed we have class together? *Two* of them!"

"What is *that* supposed to mean?" I challenged her.

"You *know* what it means." She glared at me.

Vashon waved his hand between our faces. "Hello? I don't know what it means."

Lilly's green eyes softened as she looked at her younger friend, clearly clueless. "It's really no big deal. You got some food?"

"Oh yeah, I almost forgot." Vashon jumped off the wall and jumped back on it gripping his backpack. He reached into it and pulled out two more bags of chips. He tossed one to her as he opened his own. "I got two sodas too!"

"Thanks!" Lilly didn't open her bag yet as she turned to face me. Without any trouble, she had ignored answering Vashon's question. But still, the problem hadn't gone away. I was still standing there. She was not happy. "Well, *Ozzie,* why did you walk over here?"

I frowned. "I'm not sure . . . I . . . I just saw you sitting here . . . and thought . . ."

"Wow!" Lilly smirked. "So glad you *thought.*" She pointed at the madness behind me. "You better hurry along. They don't want to leave without their *star player*." The side of her lip curled up. "That is until you *choke* again."

With his mouth full of chips, Vashon laughed, "Oh, man. Good one. Right, Ozzie?" But when he saw my face, he stopped chewing.

"I thought you weren't such a . . ."

"A what? Go on say it!" She jumped off the wall and came up to me.

"Wait! No! Don't say it." Vashon was jumping down to come between us.

But she was already looking up into my face. "You can call me all the names you want. I've heard them all." I glared down at her, but she didn't flinch at my massive size. She kept on. "But whatever it is that I am, I will claim that! But you? I bet you *still* don't know what happened last week. Do you?" I was silent. "DO YOU?"

The smell of potato chips told me Vashon had come in as close as possible. Clearly confused, he looked up at me and asked, "Do you?"

I was fuming. "What gives you the right to judge me like that! You don't know me! You aren't even from here. You come in here and act like you know everything. You and your nasty flip-flops and dirty clothes. How dare you judge me!"

"Whoa, wait. That's not right." Vashon waved his chip bag in the air. "Don't you dis my new friend like that." He finally saw that none of this was a joke. "Don't know what kind of history you two got, but—"

"We don't." Lilly stopped him and gently patted his shoulder. She hopped back up onto the wall and finally opened her second bag of chips. "Go on, play your games." She looked at me one last time. "But you see, Ozzie, the only reason I talked to you was because I thought you were different. But you're not." She started looking at the action behind me again. She looked through me. Vashon just shrugged at me and emptied the rest of his bag into his mouth.

I had been dismissed.

Chapter 16

Away

The one-hour bus ride to Delgado seemed to take forever. The pregame hype just annoyed me. If I heard, "LET THE THUNDER ROLL!" one more time, I would punch someone. Normally, I would be right there with the team. By the time we reached away games we were always pumped up and ready.

Lilly's words were like a hit to the gut. Would I really choke again? I didn't even want to look at my phone. I had avoided social media all week. I couldn't read any more posts about watching the game. Not to support the school, but to see if the Axman took a dive again. I pulled my Browns cap into my hands and touched the orange and white stitching. I didn't want to repeat last week's game. I couldn't.

Vic got up from his seat at the front of the bus and headed toward me. He made me scoot in. Two giants sharing a school bus seat must have been a sight, with his leg and half his body blocking the aisle.

"What's wrong?" He asked, but leaned in so the conversation was just between us.

"What if I choke again?" I didn't downplay my worry. It was real.

Vic didn't say anything at first. I looked at him and saw the look in his eyes. He was worried too. I dropped my head into my hands as I slipped my cap back onto my head. Great! Even my brother thought I would choke. But Vic leaned in and put his arm around my shoulders. "If you choke, then you choke. But I don't think you will." I lifted up my head and looked at him again. "You see, I learned that you do best when you have it all figured out. So, you got it all figured out this week. There will be no play that you can't handle because you are no longer trained to be excellent at a handful of brilliant plays. You are trained to be excellent at a bunch of simple plays. But, also, you know how to read plays and make your own plays." He wasn't finished. "I trained you to only listen to me, Ozzie. I trained you to follow exact directions. But when the directions changed, you choked. But that was my bad." He chuckled, "Dad made sure I understood that." I smiled. Still, he went on. "But now, Ozzie, in only one week you were able to make the shift. Not to something new, but back to something old. You always loved playing the game and could always think on your own. I took that away from you these last three years. So go back in your head to middle school and youth football."

I felt something shift. I nodded as I took in my brother's words. "Okay," was all I could say.

"Are you ready?" my brother asked.

I took a deep breath and let his words sink in. I finally looked at him and nodded, "Always!"

Vic grinned. "That's right! You are!" He squeezed my shoulder one more time as we both looked out the window. Delgado High's blue Bulldog flags lined the drive as we pulled up to the stadium.

Mom and Dad had driven down to catch the game together. It had been a while since I'd seen them both at one of my games and they both waved as Dad showed me the video camera he had hauled along, stand and all. I hoped I wouldn't disappoint them.

And I didn't. As soon as the first whistle blew, I felt it happen. Everything became clear. I felt my body react to each play as if it were made for me. My head felt free to listen and react, not react to some play in my head telling me what *should* happen. Instead, there was room to see and react to what was *really* happening.

By halftime, we were ahead 21 to 7. Vic and Coach McCoy didn't dare say a word to me, but I could see they were satisfied. They had figured out how to unleash their star player. With the roar of the crowd and my parents screaming from the sideline, I was okay with that.

That night we won 35 to 7. This time, the win included me.

Chapter 17

Homecoming

Every Friday night for the next four weeks was a replay of the game against Delgado. The chant "Axman, Axman" dominated the home *and* away games. I was on a high. It seemed that maybe I was finally feeling what it meant to *love* football. But I wasn't too sure if it was football, or the fact that I was a star that I *loved*. Maybe there was no difference.

It also helped that September's heat gave way to October's cooler days. At least cool enough to not break into a sweat every time I stepped outside. Along with football wins and the cooler weather, it helped that Zonta and I kept looking at each other. Or, in truth, I started looking at her, longer. Gavin explained that she had already been looking at me for some time, so I was finally learning how to play the game.

Our seventh game was also Homecoming. Mom and Dad both showed up and were busy catching up with old friends who had made it into town to meet old classmates and relive the "glory days". But, Dad said, they had really come to see the newest Waxman football star. I didn't disappoint. The team didn't disappoint. We played like we *were* thunder and destroyed the Franklin Lions.

At halftime, Zonta was on the Homecoming Court, stunning in her skintight, red velvet dress. She waved at the crowd and then winked at me as Silvia Hemby, a senior, was crowned Homecoming Queen.

There was always a homecoming dance after the game. I usually never went, but Gavin and Carlos had pushed me to go. So I cleaned up and wore some jeans and a fresh white T-shirt.

"Hi, Ozzie." Zonta didn't even give me a chance to walk very far into the cafeteria. She'd clearly been looking for me. The cafeteria had been transformed from a nasty lunchroom into a dance club. Or at least what I imagined a dance club would look like. Lights were flashing and some people were dancing while others were busy standing around tables filled with food and drinks. But the smell of the lunchroom was still there. It didn't matter how much you dressed up a lunchroom. It was still a lunchroom. Zonta reached her arm through the crook of my elbow and yelled, "Great game!" The music was so loud that it forced me to bend down and move in close to her face. I could feel her breath on my ear. "I said, *great game*!"

I turned my head to speak into her ear and a strand of her long, dark hair touched my cheek. "Thanks! You looked beautiful at halftime!" Then she looked at me and smiled shyly. I quickly added, "I mean. You *still* look beautiful!" Then I rolled my eyes and yelled, "I mean, you *always* look beautiful." Then I decided to just shut up. I was not good at this.

She giggled and then reached up to my ear. "Thank you, Ozzie. You don't look so bad yourself."

I nodded awkwardly. This was good, right? I wasn't so sure, but then she slipped her hand into my hand and pulled me along. I couldn't hear what she said, but I didn't really care.

She pulled me onto the dance floor and she started to move. I mean move in a way that hit me hard. Something stirred inside me as she let the music take hold of her. As her arms reached for me, I realized I had just been standing there like a creep watching her. She yelled, "Come on! Dance!"

So I did. Well, sort of. I felt the beat and moved my feet to it. I was trying not to get sweaty all over again. I had just showered and hoped my deo wouldn't let me down. And, I was very sore from the game. The simple moves were enough to make Zonta smile and keep moving like she was the only one who understood the music. She really felt it and made me want to reach for her. So I did. She let me. And by the time the music slowed, I had her up against me and she reached her arms, well her hands, around my neck and looked up at me. No words. Like she wanted me to kiss her.

So I did.

Chapter 18

Together?

It was 2 am and I had just closed my eyes. The day had been perfect. Perfect game and perfect girlfriend. At least I assumed Zonta was my girlfriend. Once I had started kissing her, I didn't stop. Or, I didn't *want* to stop. But we had to because Ms. Williams came over and made us stop. It was easy to forget it was a school dance and teachers scanned the dance floor for sketchy behavior. In fact, they kept guard everywhere, which we discovered as we tried to sneak into the corner. When Zonta had to leave, she gave me her number and we said we would talk over the weekend. The last thing she said was for me to text her.

But I didn't think she meant an hour later. My phone vibrated. There was a notification so I reached for it in the dark. I squinted at the light from the screen.

wyd

A picture of Zonta's face smiled at me. I smiled, but could barely keep my eyes open.

sleeping

how can u be when ur texting

u woke me

my bad talk later?

later is good, good night

yeah, gn

I didn't respond because I fell asleep.

I could tell it was late when I finally woke up. Mom was yelling, "Get up! I'm making breakfast for lunch. Eggs and bacon *and* some pancakes. Don't you dare make my hard work go to waste!"

I yelled back, "Coming, Mom!" The smell of bacon made my stomach growl. I could hear Vic in his room next door hurry down the hall trying to get his share before I brought my growling stomach to the table.

I found my phone next to my pillow and looked at the screen. Zonta had left 33 messages. I frowned and began to read them.

i said gn

ozzie

r u awake

hello

heeelllllooooooooooooooooooooooooooooooooooooooooo

L.B. Tillit

k i guess u r sleeping

omg still awake here

dont know how u can sleep

nevermind

r u awake now

guess i should sleep

gn

morning

so r u up yet

text me when u wake up

so its almost twelve

where r u

r u mad at me

we had a good time

well i did

i thought u did 2

do u want to see me again

did i do something wrong

is it all these texts

right

sorry

i guess we can just be friends

right

is that what u want

70

its not what i want

but if its what u want

k

bye

By the time I had read the last text I had reached the kitchen. "What is it?" Vic's mouth was full of eggs. "You look like you just missed a tackle."

I looked at Vic and shook my head. "I don't get it." I showed him my screen. He took it and read through the texts and then started laughing. "Oh, man! Welcome to the mind of a crazy woman."

Mom grabbed the phone before I could say anything and took a look herself, but she didn't laugh at me. First, she knocked Vic upside the head. "Don't you talk about women that way! You want me to tell your girlfriend what you said? I think Tamika would have some words for you! And by the way, you're a grown man still living at home with your Momma feeding you. Don't you ever talk that way again!"

"Yes, ma'am." Vic turned toward his pancakes, but as soon as Mom had her back to him, he looked at me again and twirled his finger around the side of his temple and mouthed *crazy*.

"I see you!" Mom said, which shut Vic up and let her focus on me. She handed me the phone and smiled. "Looks like this girl is crazy, yes. But crazy about you."

"What should I do?" I couldn't believe I was asking my mother. Vic shook his head too. I was clearly desperate.

"Text her." Mom said. "And I don't mean sometime today. I mean now."

So I did.

sorry just woke up i still want to be more than friends

Only a few seconds later the phone vibrated.

r u sure

yes

even after all my texts

sure

sure?

I was confused for a second, but then decided to reword.

more than sure like for real and seriously and more than anything

She responded with a smiley face and a kissing face.

I felt my stomach growl.

i need to eat talk to u later okay

okay

I finally sighed when there was no other text. I ate my pancakes, eggs, and bacon, and then an hour later the texting started all over again.

I wasn't sure what I had gotten into. Mom had said to text her, but I wasn't sure if that's what I wanted to do. At least not all day. And for sure not all weekend.

Chapter 19

What Now?

One week. It took one week of texting every day and every hour. One week of holding hands and kissing in any hiding place we could find, before I felt a shift. Her touch wasn't as exciting and the vibration of my phone made my stomach turn. It was like she was everywhere. I couldn't get away. She talked about people that didn't matter to me. Her best friend, Vonny, was being homeschooled this year while she and her family were on an RV road trip. I barely remembered Vanya Kumar, or as Zonta called her, Vonny. I had forgotten she had the one friend she did everything with. That explained why Zonta never seemed to sit with the same group of friends this year. But I thought I might lose it if she showed me one more picture or the latest text from Vonny's trip.

"What's wrong?" Zonta's voice broke into my thoughts. We were sitting alone at a table near the wall of glass, as we had all week. I looked over at the table where Gavin, Carlos and Blake were laughing and talking. I never cared before about what they talked about. In fact, I rarely listened. But suddenly, I felt like I was missing out.

I looked at Zonta and nodded at my old table. "You good with me eating with my team today? Got some team business to talk about." I lied. Guilt instantly followed. I wished that I didn't need to lie to Zonta, but I didn't know what else to do.

"Sure. We can go over there." She grabbed her tray.

"No." I said a little too quickly. "Just me, if that is okay." I forced a smile. "Don't want team secrets getting out." I was really pushing it with the lie, but she was buying it. The more she believed me, the more my guilt grew. But I told myself I was already too deep to turn back.

"Okay." She said lightly. "I'll just go sit with my friends."

"Great!" I kissed her awkwardly as I stood and grabbed my tray. "I'll text you later."

"Sure." She smiled as she stood with her tray. There was only an apple left rolling around.

I didn't let myself think about it anymore as I reached the guys' table. They each greeted me with a fist bump and we quickly started talking about our last conference game. We would be conference champs after tonight and making the playoffs was a sure thing. We dove right into talking about the State Championship and how awesome that would be. It was only when I stood up to throw away my trash that I even looked to see where Zonta had ended up. She was nowhere in the lunchroom.

As I scanned the lunchroom one more time, my eyes stopped at a table right behind the one where Zonta and I had been eating. Lilly and Vashon were sitting with about five other students I had never seen before. I guessed they were some of Vashon's freshmen friends. The only reason I stopped to look at them was because Lilly was staring at me. Not a quick look. Not a curious look. She was frowning at me. What was her problem? Pissed, I jerked my hands into the air and mouthed, "*What*?" She shook her head and then turned her head to look at something else.

I followed Lilly's gaze through the large glass wall. Zonta was sitting outside, alone. She was on her phone and biting into her apple as if nothing was wrong. The guilt that I had pushed away hit me like a brick. I pulled my phone out of my pocket to check if she had texted me. She had not. I should have felt relief, but I didn't. I didn't look in Lilly's direction again. I didn't need her judging me. I really didn't know what to do. Zonta was beautiful. She was into me and, according to the guys, she was rich. I knew I should go out there to talk to her, but I really didn't want to. So I didn't. A voice inside my head screamed,

"What is your problem?" I shoved that voice and my guilt down deep and walked to my next class. Alone.

Chapter 20

Bence

"Happy you won last night." Zonta's voice broke through my thoughts as I rode shotgun in her cosmic-blue Honda Civic. It was a sweet ride and, even though I had to push my seat all the way back in order to fit, I enjoyed the smell of new car and the sound of the engine as we drove along Hall Drive. She had picked me up and said she wanted to show me something. I was glad we weren't texting. She hadn't texted me since yesterday's lunch except to wish me luck. She must have figured out I needed some space. I took a deep breath. A ride was good. Maybe she would drive me to Midway Lake and find a private place to park. Maybe this would work out.

Mom was gone again for a few days, and Vic and Dad were on a job. Someone was moving from Newport to Hancock's upper end. It would take them all day which meant they couldn't give me crap about my girl picking me up. I could have pushed for us to take Mom's old van, but I was good with Zonta's ride.

My hopes of heading east toward the lake were dashed when Zonta turned right and headed south along Seaberg Avenue. "Where are we going?" I asked.

Zonta grinned. "Not telling. You'll see." I couldn't help but smile back. It was only a few minutes before Seaberg Avenue started to veer to the west, but Zonta suddenly turned left onto Bence Avenue. The road was lined with huge oak trees, reminding everyone of how old this neighborhood was. Their massive trunks and thick branches told their own stories. The houses that flanked their sides underwent countless changes over the years. But the oaks only seemed to grow taller and stronger. But it was not the size of the trees that I was staring at as Zonta pulled the car over to the side of the road. "See?" She barely whispered.

All I could do was nod as I took in the sun hitting the canopy of red. The oaks were putting on their final show before the leaves fell to cover Bence Avenue in a slippery mess. Carved pumpkins, fake gravestones, and random skeletons in almost every front yard, reminded me it was Halloween next week. I smiled at Zonta and said, "It's been a long time since I've been to Bence. We used to trick-or-treat here. Always had the best candy." I looked back out at the neighborhood. "Always the best candy in rich white neighborhoods, so we'd all carry pillowcases to fill up." I turned to face Zonta. "Did you ever haul off a ton of candy from here?"

Zonta lost some of her smile and nodded awkwardly as she started the car again. "I did." I held onto my Browns cap as I rolled down the window and breathed in the cool fall air. It felt good after last night's game. We were Conference Champs and playoffs started in two weeks. Maybe winter would hold off until after the championship game.

Zonta didn't say anything as we kept driving along Bence Avenue. She turned left onto Glen Avenue, with its own line of welcoming trees. As she began to drive around a bend in the road, she pulled up into a driveway. We were suddenly parked in front of a large brick house. Two garage doors were staring straight at us. A stone pathway looped around to the front door that looked like it was made out of glass. I looked at Zonta who still wasn't smiling. "Is this where you live?" I asked.

"It is." She looked at me for a minute before she added, "When I was a kid, I went trick or treating with Vonny every year. I really miss her." Zonta paused and I hoped she wasn't going to tell me the latest word from Vonny again. Instead, she added, "I brought home a ton of candy from this neighborhood because I live in this neighborhood."

I raised my eyebrows. "So, that's great!" I didn't see what was wrong at all. Her phone vibrated and she pulled it out of the cupholder to check it. I guessed it was probably Vonny again. Zonta gasped.

"Everything okay?" I asked.

She looked at me and frowned. She was just about to say something when the garage door opened. Standing in front of us was a beautiful black woman, clearly Zonta's mom. And, next to her, a tall white man started waving at me. I looked at Zonta as she pointed out the obvious. "These are my parents. They want to meet you." She looked at me and frowned a little. "I think I messed up. Again."

I didn't see what the big deal was. I didn't have time to respond before her dad had already opened my door and was shaking my hand. "Congratulations on making the playoffs." The man in front of me practically pulled me out of the car. "I'm Zeb and this is my wife, Monta."

"Hello," was all I managed before Monta came up and hugged me. I wasn't sure how to respond, so by the time I began to put my arms around her she was already backing up.

"Mom! Dad!" Zonta came up next to me. "Don't scare him." She waved at them *to go on*.

"I thought you—" Zeb's eyebrows shot up as he watched Zonta signal something and then he nodded. "Oh, okay, well . . . nice meeting you, Ozzie." Monta waved awkwardly too as she mumbled something about coming back sometime. Within a minute Zonta's parents disappeared behind the closing garage door.

I stood there staring until the door stopped groaning. With a final clank, it was silent. *We* were silent. I turned and looked down at Zonta. She was biting her nail. She was not looking at me, so I asked. "What was that about?"

"I just," Zonta hesitated. "I just wanted you to see where I lived and meet my parents. But I think it was too much." She bit her second nail.

"You think?" I kept looking at her as she tried to focus on anything but me. "I really don't get it." I waved my hand at the garage door. "That was maybe the most whack thing I've ever experienced."

Zonta dropped her hand and looked right at me. "Why? Because my dad is white and because you think I'm rich?" Her eyes began to tear up.

"What the—" I stopped and then remembered what I had said earlier. "Wait, Zonta. I don't care if your dad is white. I don't care if you're rich." I laughed out loud. "I think you being rich is great."

Zonta's eyes quickly narrowed. She was glaring. "So you only like me because you think I'm rich?"

"Wait just a minute!" I held up my hands. I looked around at the huge brick house and the silent garage doors. I couldn't believe we were doing this in front of her home. Her rich home. "I never said that!"

"It's what everyone is saying." Zonta looked away.

"Who?" I tried to reach out and touch her shoulder, but she shrugged me off.

"There are a ton of posts about it." She flung out her phone and waved it around like I didn't know what she was talking about. She was right. I didn't.

"I haven't seen any." I touched her shoulder again. This time she let me.

"But you don't check your phone like I do." She looked at me. Her anger had softened some.

"You are right about that." I laughed.

"Did your friends tell you it was good to date me because they think I'm hot and rich?" She asked me point-blank. I paused a moment too long. They had said that. It was exactly what had gone through my head. Zonta stepped back from me. Her hand went up to her mouth. "Oh my God! You *are* an ass. You are *such* an ass. Just like Carlos!"

"Wait! That's not true!" I tried to reach for her again. I liked her for her being nice too. And hot and . . . she was right.

"Are you sure?" She turned to look at me again. She had tears pouring down her face.

I couldn't lie to her. Not anymore. I dropped my eyes for a moment before I looked back up at her and whispered, "I'm so sorry, Zonta."

She didn't say anything. She walked up her perfect stone walkway and disappeared behind the glass door.

It was a long walk home.

Chapter 21

1st Period

It felt weird showing up at school Monday without Zonta quickly finding me. She didn't even look at me when I entered the room. I didn't blame her. But Lilly was staring at me from the back corner of the room, and then at Zonta, clearly making her judgment on our failed attempt at dating. I ignored them both as I settled into my seat. I checked my phone and my mouth dropped when I saw what Carlos had posted.

Axman took down Zonta. hooked up and dumped! go Axman!

I looked up and tried to get Zonta's attention, but she still didn't look at me. She had read it too. I felt heat rise. How could Carlos post this?

My thoughts were cut short when Ms. Williams finally stood up and began. "You will each be given one of the amendments in the Bill of Rights to research and present." Ms. Williams had hardly finished her sentence before the class groaned. She crossed her arms and waited for us to be quiet. "Really?" She shook her head. "Our country fought for these rights. *Your* ancestors fought for these rights and you cry about learning about them?"

"Not all our ancestors fought for these rights. Some people sitting here may not even have the same rights as us today." Blake smiled. He nodded his head at the Hispanic boy sitting in front of him. "Right, Mateo?"

Mateo's stocky frame attempted to turn around and look at Blake, but only his head could turn far enough. "You don't know anything about my ancestors! Or my rights! So shut up." Mateo's fingers reached for his earbuds. I could tell he wanted to put them in. We *all* wanted to plug our ears!

"Blake, that was not necessary." Ms. Williams was trying to keep calm.

But Blake wasn't finished. "Or Emma over there." He pointed at the only Asian girl in the room. She was sitting in front of Lilly, but I had never seen them talking. "What is your last name? Tang-something? Are you even American?"

Emma didn't even look at Blake. She barely shook her head and just stared at the teacher, clearly waiting for this to pass. Not her first time.

"BLAKE! I said stop it." Ms. Williams wasn't sure what to do. Blake's comments showed he was either that much of an idiot or he was a huge racist and we never knew it. At least, I never knew it. Suddenly, I had flashbacks to all those racist comments that ruled the lunch table. All those times I had not said anything. Did Blake really think it was okay to say those things now? I felt my face warm.

Blake shifted awkwardly as he realized most of the class was glaring at him. His eyes suddenly moved to look across the room and out the window. Anywhere but the classroom. "Come on, you all know I'm right." He really believed he was making a valid point. He needed to stop talking. Blake glanced over to Carlos and smiled. "Right, Carlos?"

Carlos' eyes went wide. "Shut up, man!" Carlos slapped the back of Blakes's head, but it was too late.

The room went completely silent. Ms. Williams started walking toward Blake and I thought she was going to knock him out. She was fuming. She was breathing heavy and her eyes narrowed.

Blake looked out the window again and dared to ask, "What? What did I say?"

"Dockins." Our teacher started. "Your last name is Dockins. It's a good chance your ancestors were still over in England when America fought for its freedom. Are you sure you aren't talking about yourself?" She took a deep breath. "Or are you only pointing out people in the classroom with a different ethnic background than you for a reason?"

Blake's face went pale. "I guess I don't really know . . . I was only thinking about history." Blake started. "I didn't mean to—"

"It *does not* matter what you *meant* or didn't mean. It is still NOT okay to question anyone's rights or anyone's ancestry. Not unless you question *every single person* in this room, regardless of race." I was waiting for Ms. Williams to kick Blake out of her class. But she started walking back to the front of the room.

I took a deep breath when Blake dropped his head and pretended to focus on his laptop. He was not going to say one more word. It was over. Carlos shook his head and decided to scoot his desk away from Blake. I didn't know if I should feel sorry for Blake or if I should hit him extra hard at practice that afternoon. I already felt like hitting Carlos for his post. One more hit wouldn't matter.

"You will have partners." Ms. Williams continued as if this racist incident had been settled. This time no one groaned. As some students began to look at each other to partner up, our teacher continued, "I will assign the partners." A few little grumbles escaped. "Blake will work with Emma." Emma's head shot up and she glared at Blake. "Her last name is Tang-Lee. Seems you need some educating. You will both take the 1st Amendment." Blake awkwardly nodded at Emma who rolled her eyes in disgust. I wondered if he would have preferred to go to the office.

As Ms. Williams called out names and classmates partnered up, I whispered under my breath *please not Zonta, please not Zonta.* Finally, she said, "Zonta, you will be with Mateo and take the 8th Amendment." I sighed, *yes, good!* But then my teacher called out my name. "Ozzie, you will partner with Lilly." *Not good.*

But it was Lilly who spoke. "Ms. Williams, can I switch with Zonta?"

Mateo looked between me and Zonta. He fiddled with his earbuds, which rested in a little pile on his desk, as he shrugged like he could care less either way. Zonta's eyes were wide and she shook her head at Ms. Williams. The teacher looked at me like she was trying to figure out why both of these girls were trying to avoid me. I smiled awkwardly. She quickly put an end to the brief exchange. "Sorry, Lilly. No changes. You two will do the 9th Amendment." She took in her whole class before she said, "It is due this Friday. So get with your partners and figure out how to make it work.

Chapter 22
It Is What It Is

Lilly gathered her stuff as slowly as possible to come sit near my table with me. She stopped to grab a textbook off the back shelf. It was an area with a bunch of books and texts we were always pushed to use, but most of us didn't bother. Then she pulled up an empty desk and adjusted and readjusted the distance between us, clearly not sure how close she wanted to be. She was the last one to settle. I stared at her. "Really? Could you move any slower?"

She raised her eyebrows. "That is a great way to start a partnership."

"Partnership is a little strong."

"Well, it is what it is. At least for a week." She opened the textbook to the back where she found *The Bill of Rights*. She shoved her long dirty blond hair over one shoulder and then leaned back in her chair to get a better look at me. Her face was blank, like she could care less.

I could already smell her. At least I was pretty sure the stale odor was coming from her. I slung open my laptop and quickly pulled it up on my search engine. "Amendment Nine, right?" I scooted my seat away from her.

"Right!" She said a little too forcefully. She knew I thought she smelled. But I didn't care. "But before we start, we got to do one thing." I pretended to look interested on my computer. She leaned over and closed my screen on top of my hands. "I *am* talking to you!"

"You just messed up my search." I fussed.

"Right." She rolled her eyes. "Really hard to find *The Bill of Rights* on the computer."

I looked at her and sighed, "What?" She shifted and then crunched up her mouth, trying to figure out how to say it. "What is it?"

"Well, we got to figure out how to do this project. Outside of class."

I hated group projects. I always ended up doing most of the work AND it still never seemed good enough. Once again, I was having to take the lead. "I'll take a part, and you take a part. Then we will each do our own thing at home. You can email me your research and I'll put it into a PowerPoint." I sighed. "Sound easy enough?"

Lilly thumbed her book for a second before her face turned red. "Not really."

"What? You want to do the PowerPoint? I really don't care who puts it together." I lied. I wanted to make sure it was perfect, but I let her think I believed she might want to do the work.

"No, you need to do the computer work. I can't." She looked at me and bit the side of her lip and then shifted her hair over her other shoulder.

It was one thing when my group said they'd do work and then end up not doing it, but she was telling me upfront she wasn't going to do it. "Wait, I'm not doing all the work!" There was no way I was going to let her get away with being lazy. Although, a part of me valued her talking straight with me, but I wouldn't tell her that.

"I'm not asking you to, idiot." She lowered her voice, "I don't have my computer. It's got to be fixed before I can use it again."

"But don't your parents have one?" I asked.

She took a deep breath. "No."

"Can't the school let you borrow one until they fix it?" I knew she had a school issued computer, like the rest of us. It didn't make sense at all.

She shook her head, trying to keep her cool. "It's complicated." She paused before she added, "Do you really want me to give you the play-by-play?"

"No, please no!" I didn't need any of her drama. I had enough of my own. "Then, I guess . . ." I didn't want to say it. "We will have to meet up somewhere."

I saw relief on her face. "Yes. Good. Anywhere."

There was no way I was going to her place. I couldn't imagine what filth she lived in. I didn't want to know. "How about 17th Street Café?" I asked. "But it would have to be after practice."

"Not a problem." She nodded.

"Then give me your number and I'll text you when I'm done." I took out my phone.

She didn't reach for her bag to pull out her phone. "No, just tell me a time and I'll be there."

I didn't care really. I didn't really want her texting me anyway. "Whatever. I can be there at 8. Pretty sure they are still open."

"I'll be there." She nodded and then we both managed to not talk the rest of the period. I looked at my computer, while she read and reread the pages in the text.

As class was ending, I dared to look at Zonta. But she didn't even glance my way. I checked my phone. She still had not texted me. I didn't blame her.

I watched Lilly pack her bag and leave without saying a word and then I looked at Blake who was avoiding everyone as he walked out the door. I told myself that at least I wasn't as bad off as Blake. Everyone thought he was a racist idiot who didn't know when to shut up. If Zonta was right, everyone thought I was a player who didn't really care about who I hooked up with. Although, we had *not* hooked up. Not even close. But I knew I couldn't tell anyone. That would make me a *real* loser.

At least I had football. At least, that's what I told myself.

Chapter 23

Fight

Football practice did not go well. We should have been on a high since we were getting ready for the playoffs. Instead, everyone was pissed. Word had spread about what Blake had said in class and half the team was ready to beat his ass. The other half kept quiet.

Carlos shoved Blake as we began to warm up. "You racist pig." Vic and coach McCoy were taking their sweet time in the locker room going over plays. Carlos was a few inches taller than Blake, and just a little heavier, but at that moment the shove caused Blake to almost fall over.

Blake found his footing and looked at Carlos, wide-eyed. "I'm not racist!" His face turned red and he looked at the ground.

"Oh, yeah?" Carlos grabbed the front of Blake's shoulder pads and pulled him up to his face. "Why did you say I didn't have a right to be in this country?"

"What? I never said that, Carlos! And you know it!" Blake was trying to pull away. "We're friends. I'd never say that about you." Most of the players stood awkwardly and didn't know what to do. Owen began to reach for Blake, but Gavin grabbed his arm and shook his head. Clearly, this was a hole Blake dug himself into. Owen shook his head and then signaled for Hunter to join him. It was only a second before Gavin followed Hunter and Owen to continue with their warm-ups. They left Blake to Carlos. A handful of players took off after the captain, but the rest stayed to watch it all play out. Including me.

Carlos shoved Blake to the ground. "You are NOT my friend. Talk trash about my people, then you are talking trash about me."

"Your people?" Blake asked. I couldn't believe it. He actually seemed confused. As four other Hispanic players gathered around him, Blakes's eyes widened. "Oh." He tried to crawl away, but one boy used his foot to shove him back down.

"Come on, let's warm up." I said the words without thinking.

Carlos turned to look at me. "What? Ozzie, are you taking this racist boy's side?" When I didn't answer he added, "You're black! Aren't you pissed?"

"I didn't say anything about black—" Blake cried out. But a kick to his stomach shut him up.

"Because I'm black you think I should be pissed, Carlos?" I said calmly, not sure why I cared if they beat Blake up. He was never someone I liked much. But something was very wrong.

"Yes, I do." Carlos's eyes flashed. He was seeing red. And he put a finger up to my face. "And you are a disgrace to *your* people if you take *his* side."

I felt heat rise. "*My* people?" I moved into his finger. "What do you know about *my* people?" Carlos found himself looking up at me as I towered over him. That familiar voice screamed in my head telling me to stop, to not draw more attention. I needed to blow this off as no big deal. But I didn't listen to that voice. I didn't move.

He held his ground. "I know *they* wouldn't put up with his racist ass."

"I'm not race—" Blake's voice was cut off again with another kick to his stomach.

That need to calm everything down finally won as I felt myself come up with a way to deal with Carlos. "You really think little, weak, pathetic Blake is a racist threat?" I pointed at the pitiful heap on the ground. Blake was quiet. "He's an idiot. We all know he's an idiot. He says stupid stuff all the time." Some of the guys began to nod. "Carlos," I tried to smile. "You have been his friend. You know what I'm talking about. He's said racist things to you before, just like you've said racist things. But everyone just laughs. Only difference is he said those things in class." I shook my head. I didn't want to face the fact that I never called anyone out on those things before. "Not so cool in front of people who might take it wrong." I wanted to say something about his nasty post about Zonta, but I didn't. I didn't want to piss off Carlos even more.

"Shut up, Ozzie." Carlos didn't like me pointing out the obvious. "You calling *me* racist?"

I was losing my own battle, again. I couldn't keep control. I moved in so close that only he could hear me. "If the shoe fits? You seem to think you got *your* people and I got *mine*." Carlos' eyes went wide.

"I said shut up!" Carlos shoved me back.

I saw red and shoved him so hard that he fell on top of Blake. He jumped up and came swinging at me, hitting me in the jaw. I swung back landing a hit against his ear. Before I knew it, we were both swapping punches as best we could with the plastic armor in the way.

"Stop it!" Vic's voice was a relief, for once. He and Coach were finally paying attention. But with one look at Gavin standing next to Vic, I knew our captain had given them a heads-up. Carlos and I stood up with busted lips, blood running from our noses and dirt on our foreheads and jerseys. "What in the hell are you two doing?" Blake slowly stood up next to me, still holding his gut. Vic shook his head and added, "The three of you?"

We didn't say anything. None of us. Vic was fuming and Coach McCoy was pacing. Finally, Coach stopped pacing and yelled, "We go to the playoffs next week and you are fighting against each other instead of with each other?" His face was so red, I thought he was going to have a heart attack. Our once-proud coach stared at us with disgust. But it was not only the three of us, he looked at every one of the players. Every player shifted awkwardly and began to look at the few strands of grass still poking out of the mostly muddy practice field. There was silence.

"Sir?" It was Blake's voice that dared to speak.

"*What,* Dockins?" Coach McCoy yelled.

"It's my fault." Blake swallowed, looking at the ground. "All of it."

Coach McCoy scratched his head. "Are you saying all of this is your fault?"

"Yes, sir." Blake suddenly held his head high, but wouldn't look directly at Coach. "They were fighting over me." Carlos and I shifted awkwardly and a couple of the players snickered. Blake looked at the players, confused.

I quickly jumped in to clarify. "We were NOT fighting *over him*. We were fighting over the stupid things he said."

Blake nodded and explained, "I split this team over racist comments, sir." He swallowed again. "Please punish me. Don't take it out on them."

Blake had just given Coach McCoy a way out. He didn't have to make two of his star players sit out any games, only his weakest player. The weakest player who took all the blame.

"Is this true?" Coach McCoy looked at Carlos and then at me. It was true. At least partly. So we both nodded. "Then go clean up and get back to practicing. And Blake, you go get cleaned up and then sit yourself on that bench. Don't expect any game time."

"Yes, sir," Blake said and quickly ran to the locker room.

Carlos and I didn't move so quickly, we both didn't know what to say to each other as we headed to the sidelines to pour water on our faces. Carlos was the first one to finally speak, "He *is* an idiot."

I nodded. "Yes, he *is*."

We were ready to move on.

Chapter 24
The 9th Amendment

There were only a handful of people at 17th Street Café. It wasn't as popular as Starbucks across the street, which was one reason I chose it. The less people saw us together, the better. I also didn't want to answer any questions about practice. I was sure word had already spread.

Lilly waved at me from across the half-empty café. I nodded at her and bought a muffin and large iced coffee before I joined her. Lilly watched me put down my drink, swallow my muffin in two bites, and take off my Browns cap, before she asked, "Rough practice?"

"Yep!" was all I said. It was enough. She didn't push for any more details. Instead, she pulled out her book and notes from her backpack and sat next to me at the table. She was trying to look at my computer at the same time. I was trying to ignore how awkward it was for her to be close, especially since her stale odor was strong. I shifted once, taking a long sip from my drink, hoping she would back off a little. She did. Thankful for a little space, I focused on the words on my screen. I shook my head at what I was reading. "What in the world does this mean? *The enumeration in the Constitution, of certain rights, shall not be construed to deny or disparage others retained by the people*." I thought this was going to be easy.

"Wait a minute." Lilly moved even further away from me to read a place she had marked in her textbook and then looked at me. "*Enumeration* basically means *listed*, or like *numbered*."

"Okay, and?" My head was hurting from practice. I was sore and hungry. The muffin I had scarfed down was not enough. I'd eat what was left over from dinner when I got home. But I dreaded facing Vic and whatever he had to say. I knew it wasn't over.

Lilly's voice broke into my thoughts. "And it's talking about all the rights listed in the Constitution." She actually seemed excited. "So, *construed to deny*, means it shouldn't be like *twisted to explain*. AND *disparage others retained by the people* basically means *criticize* or like somehow *undermine* the *rights the people already have*."

"So you are saying that this one Amendment basically says that all the other rights listed are not supposed to take away from the rights we have already?" It was slowly making sense.

"Yes, Ozzie." It was the first time she said my name in a long time without sounding pissed. She thought a second. "So just because the

Bill of Rights doesn't list that you have a right, like, to be able to learn to drive, then that doesn't mean it is NOT a right." She frowned. "Or something like that, I think."

"That makes sense." I laughed. "My brother and I used to try to get away with stuff like that all the time at home. Like the one time I wore his new shirt because Mom had put it with my clothes. Vic claimed I had stolen it, but I told her we didn't have any rules to say that I couldn't wear his clothes if they were in *my* closet. Mom screamed at me that just because we didn't have a rule about it, didn't mean it was any less his shirt." I smiled. "Basically, he still had a right to his shirt."

Lilly's green eyes lit up and her smile grew as she got all excited. "Okay, so that means we have to come up with a way to present this to the class. But maybe a better example than stealing your brother's shirt."

"Hey!" I began, but then saw she was teasing. "I wasn't stealing!"

"Says who? I think your brother was right."

I laughed. "Okay, okay . . . so different examples."

We were both totally into figuring this project out. Together.

Chapter 25

Wrong

We spent the next hour working through ways to present the 9th Amendment to the class, and I found myself completely engaged in conversation. We shot out ideas, disagreed, agreed, and compromised until we had our plan ready.

A couple of times Lilly came in close. Her stink made me shift away. But her green eyes and intensity always drew me back in. I even thought that she might be pretty if she cleaned herself up. Then suddenly I'd shift away again. I tried not to be obvious, since we were working well together. But still, I was pretty sure she noticed.

"I've got to go." I felt lightheaded. "I'm starving."

"Okay," Lilly said a little too quickly and began to put her book in her backpack.

I frowned. "Are you good?"

"What?" She stood up and began to sling the bag over her shoulder.

"I really *am* hungry and need to get home." I wanted to make sure she knew it had nothing to do with her smell, but without actually saying it.

She nodded awkwardly. "I'm sure you are."

"Something wrong?" I asked as I closed my laptop.

Lilly shook her head. "Nope. All good." She paused and hesitated a minute. "Are you going to finish that drink?"

I looked at the large half-finished iced coffee. All the ice had melted, leaving a sweet mushy mess. "No." I answered. My eyebrows lifted. "Do you *want* it?"

"Sure! Thanks." She grabbed it and turned to leave.

I shoved my laptop in my backpack, grabbed my Browns cap, and quickly followed her out the door. "Wait." The street was still busy with Pizza World and Hancock Burger nearby. The sudden whiff of fast food made my stomach growl even more. Lilly turned to face me as I caught up. "Did I say something wrong?" Suddenly she took a long sip of my drink and I couldn't help but cringe.

Lilly stared at me with that old look again, one I hadn't seen for the last hour. "I'm not sure what your problem is? You said you needed to go, and I said okay, and we both left. No problem." Her eyes hardened as she added, "Or . . . do you want your drink back?"

"No, no!" I quickly said, taking a step back. "It's yours now." I stared at her and tried to figure out what her game was. It was some twisted game. She didn't back down and gave me an intense look. It wasn't mean or angry. She looked like she could care less. "I don't get it," I admitted. I waved at the coffee shop behind me. "One minute you are the best project partner I have ever had, and the next minute it's like you could care less about everything."

For one second, I saw a flicker in Lilly's eyes. I had struck something. She was holding herself together, determined not to respond. I shook my head and gave up. As I turned to head to the bus stop, I heard her scramble up next to me. So I looked at her again as she finally spoke. "Thanks, Ozzie," her voice broke.

I turned my body to face her. "What is wrong, Lilly?"

She quickly wiped her eyes with her sleeve. Trying to shake it all off. "I can't tell you." I waited for her to say more. But she just shook her head. "I got a lot going on. Trust me. You don't want to know." She began to back away. Wiping her face again. Taking a deep breath, she managed a chuckle. "Best project partner? Really?" She took another sip of my iced coffee.

I smiled and nodded. "Really."

"I promise next time I won't stink." She teased.

My eyes went wide. "I didn't notice."

"You suck at lying." She laughed awkwardly. "You'll see. I'm not always this way."

"What way?" I asked.

She shook her head. "Seriously, stop pretending I don't disgust you."

I dropped my eyes. "You don't."

"There you go again." Her voice wavered. "Liar!" I looked back up and she was staring at me. I could literally see a thought form. A plan. "You'll see!"

My bus pulled up. By the time I was in my seat, Lilly had disappeared. I felt my stomach drop again, like the last time I left her at a bus stop. Should I have pushed her to tell me what she was talking about? I could still see her eyes. There had been a spark of fear. As the bus pulled away, I told myself Lilly was just too much. I had tried to be nice, but she didn't believe me. My stomach turned again. Why should she believe me? She was right, I was lying. I pushed that surge of guilt away. I shoved it down deep. None of it really mattered, so I tried not to think about Lilly anymore.

Chapter 26

Another Lie

I was shoveling as much leftover beef stew into my mouth as possible as Vic tore into me. "What did you think you were doing at practice? You could have hurt your hands. You might have already hurt your hands."

"My hands are fine." I lied. They were a little sore and I could feel a bruise forming along the knuckles on my right hand. I shoved another spoonful of stew into my mouth. I wanted to eat and go to bed as soon as possible and end this unbelievable day.

"This is NOT funny, Ozzie!"

"I'm NOT laughing!" I glared at him, still chewing since I had no desire to sit there and take his lecture.

"You think you are going to win this championship fighting your own players?" He was pacing and acting like the parent of the house, since Mom was out of town again and Dad was already asleep.

"It's over." I stated as a matter of fact. I wasn't going to start explaining to my brother how part of the problem was that I never stood up to Carlos before. I hoped that was the first and last time. At least the team saw the whole fight as two tough guys settling their differences. Problem was, Blake took all the blame. That part kept eating at my gut.

Vic stopped pacing and came to sit across from me at the kitchen table. "Is it, Ozzie?" I just shrugged. "Exactly! You don't KNOW if it is over."

"It felt over," I suggested. It made sense that if we all pretended hard enough it *could* be over.

"Felt?" Vic took a deep breath and rubbed his hands over his face. "That's the problem. You *felt* it was okay to hit Carlos."

"He started it." I suddenly felt like a six-year-old. The more I talked the worse it got.

"Really, Ozzie?" Vic wasn't letting up. "It feels like you really don't care about winning the state championship."

I put down my spoon and reached for my glass of milk. "I do care."

"But do you want it?" Vic challenged me. "Do you really want it?"

"You mean like you?" I shot right back at him.

Vic paused a minute and took a breath. "Yeah, like me."

I didn't answer right away. I drank my whole glass of milk, buying time. The truth had finally been spoken. My brother had always wanted it more than me. Always. But I didn't want to confess that to him or to anyone. So I finally said, "Of course I do." But it was too late. He knew.

He stood up from the table and looked at me one last time. A deep sadness hung in the air. "Good. That's what I want to hear." He also wasn't ready to let go of the lie.

Chapter 27

Missing

I was thankful when Tuesday and Wednesday felt normal at school. At least somewhat. At lunch, we all still sat together. Gavin made sure of it. He told all of us we had to show we were a united team. Carlos and Blake acted like nothing had happened, but Blake's silence and fake laughs told me he was watching his every word and move. Carlos and I would glance at each other's bruised face and then just nod. We were both trying to prove we could move on. Gavin tried to steer the conversation to next week's playoff game. Everyone was willing to let him set the mood.

Zonta continued to ignore me, even when we accidentally walked through the door at the same time on Tuesday. I backed off and let her through first. She nodded politely, but that was it. Then on Wednesday she walked by my table, stopped for one second, like she was going to say something, but moved on without a word. Strange. I told myself it was better to let it go.

It was Thursday before I realized that Lilly hadn't been at school for three days. At first, I thought she was late to school as she tended to be. But when she didn't even show up for first *and* second period for three days, I started to wonder. We were going to present our project on Friday and even though we had finished it on Monday night, I still thought she would want to go over it at least one time before Friday.

At lunch, I left my tray of food at my table and then walked across the lunchroom to a long table crowded with freshmen. I saw Vashon laughing at some pictures on his phone with a couple of friends. Of course, they noticed me towering over them before he did. "Vashon!" I tried to sound calm.

Vashon's eyes grew wide and then his smile followed. "Hey, Ozzie! What's up?" His freshman friends seemed impressed, and Vashon was soaking it up.

"Can we talk?" I asked. Vashon quickly jumped up, not needing me to explain that I meant *in private.*

"Sure!" Vashon followed me a few feet away from the table and, for a moment, I caught Gavin and Carlos looking at me from across the room wondering what the heck I was doing.

I lowered my voice. "Where is Lilly?"

Vashon looked around the room. "Is she not here?"

"I thought she ate with you."

Vashon shook his head. "Sometimes. But sometimes I don't see her for days." He frowned. "Why? What's wrong?"

"We have a presentation tomorrow and she hasn't been to school since Monday." I wasn't sure why I was telling this to Vashon, but I needed to say it to someone. Anyone who might care.

Vashon nodded as his eyes narrowed. "So, you're pissed she's not helping you?"

I frowned. "No, that's not it." I realized he had only seen Lilly and me hating on each other. "I'm just . . . worried."

A laughed escaped from Vashon. "Oh, man! That's funny."

"What's so funny?" I felt my heat rise.

"Listen, Ozzie, Lilly can take care of herself." He slapped my shoulder. "Don't worry about her. She'll be back around." He looked to the table where one of his friends was leaning over his food and then yelled, "Hey, man! Don't touch my fries!" And one second later he was gone, fighting over his lunch tray.

By the time I had returned to my own lunch tray, my fries were gone too. Gavin gave me a smirk and expected me to grab the heaping fries off his tray, obviously my missing portion. But I just tried to eat my two burgers and think about where Lilly might be. I knew nothing about her world and couldn't even guess if she was okay or not. Although her behavior on Monday night did tell me something was not right. My stomach turned again and I couldn't eat. I hoped she would show up in the morning.

But she didn't. I gave our presentation without her and wondered why Ms. Williams didn't even ask why Lilly wasn't helping me. Even though she didn't ask, I explained how Lilly figured out the meaning of the amendment. Ms. Williams nodded with interest and took notes, like Lilly was there with me. Strange. I barely paid attention to the other presentations. The only one that caught my attention was Blake and Emma's presentation, only because Emma did all the talking and Blake barely looked at the class. Ms. Williams seemed satisfied enough. Blake would think very carefully about how he expressed himself in the future.

I looked toward the back of the room to where Lilly's seat sat empty. Was I really the only one who wondered where she was? Was I the only one who thought something was strange? Was I the only one who noticed she was missing?

Chapter 28

Questions

It felt strange not having a game that Friday, but we were all thankful for an extra week to prep for the first play-off game. The week before the big game, practices were intense, but good. We all worked hard at showing Vic and Coach McCoy that we were one as a team, even if some of us were faking it. Blake kept busy as a water boy and didn't even bother putting on his practice jersey. He brought us water during practices and picked up our towels off the locker room floor. The whole time, nobody said anything to him. We all moved through the week as if Blake had always been our water boy. But he never complained and he showed up every day. A few times he caught me looking at him, but he quickly looked away. Ashamed, but not broken. I found myself laughing at myself, because it was the first time that the idiot didn't annoy me. He was growing on me.

That Thursday, first period, class hadn't started yet, so the usual talk filled the room. I sat down at my desk as always, but suddenly the class became quiet. I looked up and saw Zonta had stopped in the doorway with Lilly standing next to her. Lilly wore a clean blue sweater over a white tank top and had some black leggings on. She looked smaller. Her flip flops were gone and she was wearing some black ankle boots. Her hair looked clean, but it was hanging down, loose over her face. She was clearly trying to cover the left side of her face, but we could all still see the yellow tint of her skin. The final fade of two dark purple spots also peaked through. There was one under her eye and one along her jawline. Ms. Williams jumped up to go talk to her out of ear shot. Zonta stayed next to Lilly. She didn't want to move away from her, but Lilly gave her a short nod. With one final look, Zonta gave in and headed to her own desk. The teacher took her time listening and nodded as Lilly shared the details.

As Lilly walked past my desk she stopped and looked down at me. Her green eyes stood out against her bruises. "I'm sorry I missed our presentation. I heard you did a good job!"

"No big deal." I didn't know what to say. I had so many questions. Who would do this to her? Nobody asked or worried about Carlos's and my fat lips and bruises, but this was different. "What happened?" I asked. But the class was still trying to listen, even with a few people beginning to whisper.

Lilly shook her head and glanced around at all the eyes on her before she looked back at me. "It's a long story, and, besides . . . I don't think you really want the play-by-play."

I didn't get a chance to respond before she headed back to her seat. The class went on, once again, like nothing had happened.

But something had happened. At lunch, Zonta and Lilly were sitting together. They weren't laughing or looking at their phones, but they were talking and eating. Although Lilly was clearly struggling with chewing. I knew I should at least be happy that Lilly had made a friend in her own grade. But Zonta? She was someone who didn't even want to talk to me anymore. I would never find out what happened.

I told myself to let it go. I really shouldn't care. But then I started to wonder if I was somehow responsible? I had left Lilly at the bus stop on Monday night knowing something was wrong. Did that fear I saw in her eyes mean she was in danger? Was she hurt because of me? Because I wasn't honest with her? I knew Zonta was hurting because of me . . . because I couldn't be honest with others about what happened, or really *didn't* happen, between us. What kind of monster was I? I had nowhere to go with my thoughts so I did what I did best. I pushed them all deep down.

Chapter 29

1st Playoff Game

The cool fall breeze welcomed us as we marched out onto the field. It was at home, which was great. All our home fans spilled into the stands and waved black flags featuring white lightning bolts. Mom told me she would come to the state championship game, but had to work the weekends during the playoffs. I didn't worry about it. As long as she came to our championship game, I was happy. I never doubted we would be champions.

Dad waved from the stands with his phone. He still recorded everything I did, even if it was just so he could relive the plays on his own, especially when he wanted to show a complete stranger a favorite clip. Schools and Universities didn't need any more footage from us. At least ten top schools had contacted Coach McCoy. They had watched all the school's video footage and were emailing me and sending me letters. As a junior, I already had my pick of where I wanted to go to college.

As we neared the benches on our side of the field, I started thinking about how Vic wasn't quite as excited when he saw the letters and emails arrive. Dad fussed at him, once yelling, "Come on, Vic! Aren't you happy for Ozzie?"

Vic had responded, "I am, Dad. I really am." But one glance at me told me everything. He wished it was him, at least *he* would want it. *He* was the one who wanted a big football career.

I did want it. At least that's what I told myself. I did want to go to school, and I wanted to play ball. But Vic's look reminded me that I didn't want it as badly as he did. I let the doubt begin to seep back in. That huge part of me that didn't want to leave my Hall neighborhood, or Hancock, screamed that I could never make it out there. Away. Alone.

I was jolted away from my thoughts as the screaming fans in the stands reminded me of the part I did love. I loved hearing the chant. "Axman, Axman, Axman." I breathed it in and let it fill me. I was not alone. Not yet.

"Make it mean something." Vic's voice hit me like a brick. He was standing behind me as we were lining up for the national anthem.

I turned to face him. "It always means something." How dare he take this moment away.

Vic snorted. Piped in music blared as we listened to Mateo belt out the national anthem. I didn't know he could sing. I hoped Blake was paying attention. As soon as he was finished and the crowd roared, Vic looked at me. My pissed brother was gone. He was my coach again as he asked, "You ready?"

I let everything go and nodded. "Always."

Vic slapped my shoulders. "That's right. You are!" He turned and left me so he could pump up the rest of the team.

The first half was a beast. The Hemby Hawks had made the playoffs and were a stronger team than when we played them last. Their red helmets hit me over and over again. But it wasn't just me. Gavin was sacked three times, and our running backs, Carlos and Hunter, could barely break past the line of scrimmage. But we still put the first points on the board. Even if it was just three points. By half time it was only 3 to 0.

We were exhausted and there was little talk in the locker room at half time. Blake quickly made sure we all had water. He also picked up any dirt and blood-smeared towels we threw on the floor. Coach McCoy didn't take his time getting to the locker room. Pats on the back and catching up could wait until after the game. "We are not going to lose this game," he said calmly. We all listened and moved our sore bodies like old men. "You have forgotten what it means to fight for your win. You have forgotten what it means to push yourselves. It's been too easy." He shook his head. "BUT here is the thing. You *are* the best." He looked at each one of us. "The question now is if you want to go all the way. Do you want this?"

"Yes." We answered.

"I said, DO YOU WANT THIS?" He yelled.

We jumped up and yelled, "YES!"

We meant it. I meant it.

The Hemby Hawks made us work for every yard, but the Hancock Thunder did not back down. With 1 minute left on the clock, we were fourth down on the 10-yard line. We could kick again, but it was our only chance to get a touchdown. I looked at Carlos, Gavin, and Owen. We knew what we needed to do. As soon as Gavin took the snap, he handed it off to Carlos who began to run the ball with Owen and me paving the way. Only a few yards left and Carlos passed me by while Owen flanked his other side. Just as Carlos crossed into the end zone, a Hemby Hawk dove at my legs. I felt my right knee pop. Intense, sharp pain took over as I hit the dirt. I grabbed my knee and screamed as the stadium cheered for the first, and only touchdown of the game.

We won, but I was carried off the field and straight to the hospital.

My ACL was torn.

Any hope of playing in the state championship game was crushed.

With more playoff games to come, I hoped my team could get to the championship without me, but I seriously doubted they could pull it off. They needed me.

Chapter 30

Rift

Resting, icing, and elevating my knee was how I spent the rest of that weekend. I was pissed that I had to stay stretched out on the living room couch. A bandage compressed the injury some, but the swelling was still bad. Learning to use my new crutches was not fun, when all I wanted was to celebrate with the team. The closest I came was reading or watching posts. But I had to put down my phone after ten posts replayed my fall from different angles. And there was the fact that Owen's post *the Axman chopped down* got over two hundred *likes* in one hour.

A few guys stopped by to check on me Saturday, but they were headed to the lake for a cookout. A few fist bumps later they were out the door telling me to hang tough. They promised to bring me some hotdogs, but they never did.

Mom finally got home Sunday night. She fussed over me and served chocolate ice cream with the works. The TV had been on all day with

NFL games taking my mind off my pain. The ice cream was a bonus. Dad had just returned to his recliner with his own bowl when Vic walked through the door. He had spent the weekend with Tamika "celebrating."

"So, how is the knee?" Vic asked. He looked worried but was trying to sound relaxed.

Before I could answer, Dad jumped in. "Doc says he can't do surgery yet. The swelling has to go down and he has to do physical therapy for at least the next three weeks."

Vic nodded. "Okay, that sounds good."

Dad scooped up a mouthful of ice cream. "I think so."

"Means he could be ready for next season. With rehab on the other side of surgery." Vic was talking to himself more than anything.

"He's a Waxman! I know he'll be ready!"

"I'm sitting right here!" I yelled.

Mom raised her eyebrows. "Ozzie, honey, no need to yell. They were just talking . . ."

"*Just talking* is right." I shifted and felt a sharp pain. I groaned. Vic ran over to help me get my knee elevated again. I shoved him away. "Get off me."

"Ozzie," Mom looked between Vic and me. "I don't know what's wrong, but you two better figure it out." She got up and headed into the kitchen.

Vic frowned at me. "Yeah! What's your problem?"

"My problem?" My mouth dropped. "Really? Do you not see my knee is trashed and you act like I just fell off my bike? You are talking like getting over this is no big deal."

"Oh," Vic sucked air through his teeth. "So you're feeling sorry for yourself?" I shook my head and wouldn't answer. "Big baby sitting on the couch, eating his ice cream."

"Vic, that's enough," Dad spoke softly.

"Is it, Dad?" Vic turned to face our father. "I really think you and Mom baby him too much."

"Is that right?" Mom couldn't help herself, as she came back around the corner. *Staying out of it* was not her style. "Who is a grown man, working a job, coaching, and still lives at home with his parents? You! AND you get to go and crash at your girlfriend's place when you want. Then when you get tired of her, you come running home to your Momma's cooking."

"Don't flatter yourself, Mom! We're lucky if we get a home-cooked meal from you once every one or two weeks. You know Dad's the one who's been raising us."

"Vic! Do NOT speak to your mother that way!" Dad was fuming.

Mom shook her head in disgust. "Oh really? You won't even be that lucky from now on. You go and get your stuff out of your room. Out of MY house. And move in with Tamika. See how fast you grow up!"

"Come on, Mom." Vic's voice softened. "You don't mean that." She stood with her arms crossed and stared him down. He looked to Dad. "Dad, tell her to calm down. This isn't that serious. She can't just kick me out."

Dad looked at Mom who didn't take her eyes off Vic. "The truth is, Vic, we should have kicked you out a long time ago." I couldn't believe what I was hearing. I wanted Vic to be chewed out, but being kicked out was too much. Still, I didn't say a word. It had started with fighting about me. I didn't want to make it worse.

"What's that supposed to mean?" Vic was beginning to pace.

"It means you have told us for three years now you would get your own place. And you told us you would help with bills until you moved out. But you haven't done either of those things. We have made it too easy for you." Dad explained.

Mom jumped in. "That's what happens when we baby our boys too much! I thank you for pointing that out!"

"Come on! That's not fair. That's NOT what I meant. You've got to let me stay." Vic begged.

Mom's eyes softened, but she held firm. "Vic, I love you, but you have until the end of this week to move out." She turned and went back into the kitchen. We could hear her cursing up a storm. Dad pushed himself out of his recliner, holding his bowl, and followed her. It was only seconds before we heard Mom crying and Dad whispering soft words to comfort her.

I looked at Vic with eyes wide open. "What the hell was that?"

Vic shook his head. And then he glared at me. "Thanks a lot, Ozzie!"

I tried to sit up, but the throbbing in my knee kept me down. "What did I do?"

"Nothing!" Vic answered. "Absolutely nothing! You sat there and didn't stand up for me." He looked at me one more time before he headed out the front door.

I was suddenly alone with my throbbing knee. Alone on the couch, with the TV blaring and a bowl full of melting ice cream. What had I done? What had just happened to my family?

Chapter 31

Back to School

Heading back to school with crutches wasn't too bad. There were several girls willing to help me carry my backpack and I felt somewhat like a hero. I guess *the Axman chopped down* wasn't as awful a post as I thought it was.

When I sat down at my desk-table in first period, I propped my leg up on a chair. Carlos and Blake walked past me, each giving me a high five. But it was Lilly who stopped. She looked at my leg and her eyes narrowed. Her bruises were barely visible so she was wearing her hair pulled back. "What happened to you?"

I was surprised by her question. "I tore my ACL at the game. Thought everyone knew."

"Well, excuse me!" she smirked. "We don't all follow social media."

I lifted my leg to shove my jacket under it. "I didn't mean anything by it." She didn't move on, so I dared to ask her again. "So, what happened to you?"

She quickly shook her head. "Not anything I can't handle." She blew me off again. Then she actually touched the bandage on my leg. "Looks like you got your own worries." As she turned and headed to her seat, the reality of the situation hit me. I did have a lot to worry about. I had no idea if I could ever recover from the ACL tear to play football again, at least as well as I had before. But the reality was I didn't know if I had it in me. Didn't know if I wanted it badly enough. Never wanted it as badly as Vic did.

Class still hadn't started, so I checked my phone and saw I had a text. It was from Zonta. I looked at her across the room and she nodded at me and then pointed to her phone. So I read her text.

r u ok?

I looked at her, but she was looking at her phone, so I responded.

torn ACL

that sucks

for sure

can u play football

not for a while

hope u get better soon

thanx I paused, but then added *r u ok*

I looked up to see if she would answer. She looked at me and smiled. Just a little smile. Ms. Williams entered the room and the conversation was over. But I felt some relief. It was the most she had said to me in two weeks. Maybe she would be ready to talk again. Maybe.

Chapter 32

The Truth

When class was over, I made a point to swing myself over to Zonta's locker.

"Hi, Zonta." I said awkwardly.

She was clearly surprised to see me. "Ozzie?" She grabbed her book from her locker before she closed it. "Everything okay?"

I leaned heavily on my crutches and could feel my knee throbbing. I needed to get to second period and prop it up again. But I had to talk to Zonta. Her texting me told me she was willing to talk again, at least that was what I read. But when I saw the frown on her face, I started to doubt my take on her reaching out to me. "I thought maybe . . . since you texted . . . maybe . . . you—"

"Stop right there, Ozzie." Zonta was still frowning. "I texted you because I was worried. Not because I want to start talking again." She looked around at the stares we were beginning to get. At least two or three girls looked at Zonta like she was trash. "And I, for sure, don't want people to think we hooked up *again*." She pretended to be thinking. "Wait, we never did hook up, did we?"

"No, Zonta. I'm sorry . . ." I began.

"But no one else knows that, do they, Ozzie?" She began to turn away.

"Wait. What about Lilly?" I asked.

She turned and looked at me. "What about Lilly?"

I shifted to my left, hoping to stop the throbbing, but it didn't help. "You seem to be friends. What happened to her? She won't tell me anything."

Zonta walked up to me and got really close. "What do you think happened, Ozzie?" She whispered so no one else could hear. "That night you two worked together she tried to go to her aunt's house to take a shower. But her aunt's no-good boyfriend was there and beat the crap out of her." She shook her head. "I couldn't believe she called me. But she did."

"I don't get it? Why go to her aunt's house and not home?"

Zonta's eyes opened wide. She was surprised, again. "Ozzie, really?"

"What?" I was sweating now.

She looked almost sorry for me as she explained, "Ozzie, Lilly is homeless. She crashes where she can. Right now, she's at our place."

I didn't say a word. Zonta saw how shocked I was and left me to deal with my own thoughts. The bell rang, and I quickly found myself alone in the hallway. I slowly made my way down the hall, each step harder to take than the last. Pain shot through me and my hands were beginning to cramp against the crutches. They were not used to carrying my massive bulk. But I didn't care. I deserved the pain. If I hadn't let Lilly know that I thought she stunk or that I thought she was disgusting, she would never have tried to go shower at her aunt's house. She would never have been beaten up. What kind of monster was I?

I thought I could push past my regrets. I was sure that letting the rumor spread about Zonta and me hooking up was no big deal. But the looks the others gave her in the hall told me *she* had suffered. Not me.

Not standing up to Carlos' comments in the lunchroom caused Blake to think racist comments and awful stereotyping were okay, but then he was beaten up and benched for the rest of the season. Because of me, Blake wouldn't get to fight for the championship. All Blake ever did was look up to me, and I let him down.

Then there was Vic. My brother. I couldn't even open my mouth to stand up for my own brother. I was such a loser!

As I reached second period, the teacher didn't call me out for being tardy. The crutches and the sweat pouring down my face said it all. I managed to slide into my seat and prop up my leg, but I still couldn't hear what the teacher was talking about. I turned my head across the room to look at Lilly. She was staring at me, confused. I held her stare as tears filled my eyes and I shook my head and mouthed *I'm sorry*. Shock filled her eyes as her hand went up to her mouth. She knew I knew.

I looked away and wiped my eyes with my sleeve, and tried to push every one of my mistakes as deep down as possible. If I tried hard enough, I could push it away and move on.

Chapter 33

The Dive

The next three weeks were a blur. Playoffs seemed to be going well without me. I should have been happy for my team, but I found myself fading into the background. Hunter and Owen had become regulars at the lunch table where Gavin and Carlos were consumed with replaying wins and talking about new plays. Ones they had to create because I was gone. Ones that were going so well because no other team expected them. They were better off without me. Blake seemed to be finding his way back, but once in a while, he'd glance my way and frown. He'd ask me if I was okay and I would blow him off, giving him some lame excuse. He would nod and smile like he believed me and then move on.

Coach made me come and sit on the bench during the games. It was what injured players did. But something happened during those late nights. The lights were bright and the screaming intense. But no one chanted "Axman". I had not realized how much I lived for those moments. I loved the energy. The intensity. I loved being looked up to. I had been the star lineman. But I was suddenly a nobody. I suddenly didn't matter. Just like that. My head hurt trying to make sense of it. How could I not love football but still love all that energy? What was wrong with me? Maybe it was what kept me in the game. It was how I told myself that Dad and Vic were right and that it was in my blood. But those moments of being at the top were gone. Those times I held onto football, because it was somehow worth it, were gone. I felt a numbness crawl inside my head. A numbness that felt right.

The numbness deepened as my home shattered even more. Vic hadn't spoken to me since he moved into Tamika's place. She wasn't too happy, but that was their problem. Mom and Dad didn't say much and we all pretended like it was good we had the extra room. More space for me to do my exercises. But all talk of a football comeback had faded and I didn't care, so I didn't try too hard to get better. Mom seemed to find ways to be gone longer and Dad had the TV blaring all the time. Thanksgiving was just another day watching TV. No turkey, no Mom, no Vic.

Zonta and Lilly avoided me. Or maybe I avoided them. I tried not to say anything to anybody. I really didn't want to be there. Nobody really wanted to talk to me, and I really didn't want to talk to anyone else.

Surgery was supposed to be at the end of the first week in December. The same week as the championship game. I didn't want to face either. Not because I was afraid. I just didn't care.

It was the Monday before Saturday's championship game and two days before my knee surgery. I had finally mastered moving around with my crutches. I had made a plan. That voice in my head told me that it was about time I did something. Something that would make sure I never let anyone else down or cause any more pain. My thoughts didn't seem dark or even scary. They were just dull and flat. A clear sort of logic led the way. A logic that allowed me to feel nothing.

It was early in the morning, before first period. I found Blake in the hall and pulled him aside. "Blake, I got something for you."

Blake smiled at me. "Hi, Ozzie. What is it?"

I didn't smile back. I reached into the side pocket of my backpack and pulled out my Cleveland Browns cap. I handed him the one item that, up to that moment, I had loved the most. But the hat only felt like a strange object in my hand. An object that Blake deserved more than I did. "I want you to have this."

Blake smiled and took the cap. "Wow! Thanks, Ozzie." He put it on his head and adjusted the fit. "So cool!" He pulled it on and off his head three times before he asked. "Are you going to get yourself a new one?"

I shrugged. "We'll see."

Blake nodded and waved at Carlos who was walking by. "Hey, Carlos, look what Ozzie gave me!" Carlos tried to grab the hat, but Blake dodged out of the way in time.

"Hey, Ozzie. Got something for me before the championship game?" He smiled.

I shook my head. "No, man. You don't hurt for anything. You already have all the magic you need." I forced a smile. It felt strange.

Carlos began strutting. "You're damn right I do!" Carlos and Blake kept moving down the hall making as much pregame noise as possible. Even if it was only Monday.

I found Zonta's locker and slipped a note into it. Since I didn't know where Lilly's locker was, I slipped in a note for her too. I told them both I was sorry and hoped they could forgive me.

Then I left the school. I decided to take bus 66 on home. I waited on the bench for the 9:16 am bus. It was the same bench I had first pushed Lilly away. First been disgusted with her. I didn't even know or care to know that she was homeless. The guilt had eaten at me for so long. But at that moment, I didn't even feel the guilt anymore. It was a strange memory.

Dad and Vic would be working and Mom wasn't going to be home until my surgery. I would be alone. I had several pain pills left over from the first week after my ACL tore. I hadn't used many, which left me with enough. Enough to move on. To let everyone be rid of me. I was worthless and a burden.

They were done with me. I was done with me.

Chapter 34

Failure

The bus ride home felt long. I watched the familiar buildings and streets pass by. I didn't really feel sad. I didn't really feel anything much since that guilt that I held onto for so long had melted away. I was simply numb.

It was only 9:45 am when I got off the bus. I swung myself down Hall Drive, trying to avoid making eye contact with anyone.

"Ozzie Waxman?" A voice yelled. I looked up and was surprised to see Mrs. Wilkes across the street at Hall Grocery. She waved for me to stop and walked across the street toward me. I didn't dare move another inch. I hadn't seen Vashon's grandma in so long, but I would recognize her white-streaked hair anywhere. She looked like a rock star. An old one. "Why aren't you in school, Ozzie?"

I couldn't believe this was happening. Of all days for Mrs. Wilkes to be in my business! I took a deep breath as the old lady finally reached me. "Got to get home. Knee's bothering me." I lied. I began to shuffle ahead. But the old lady's arm reached out and stopped me. Her touch made me flinch. I moved my arm away. I couldn't have anyone touch me. It would ruin everything. I was not worthy of touch. I did not deserve to feel like someone cared. I didn't want to feel anything.

Mrs. Wilkes' eyes narrowed. "Is that so?" She looked me up and down. "Looks like you are getting along fine." I started to move away from her, again. "I'm not done talking to you, boy!" I stopped and looked at her, shocked to hear her talk to me like I was ten again. She had no problem whooping my butt then. It seemed she would have no problem doing it now, even with me standing like a giant next to her. "Seems all Vashon does is talk about how he wants to be like you."

My eyebrows rose. "Really?" Something began to give. My voice inside me screamed to stop looking at her, to stop listening. It was all a lie. How could Vashon even look up to me? How could anyone still look up to me? I was a nobody!

Mrs. Wilkes grinned and then put a hand gently on my forearm, again. This time I did not move away. The warmth from her hand soothed something deep inside. "That's right, Ozzie. Now, don't you forget that when you go on home and skip school." She lifted her hand and then shook her finger at me. "Don't want any of my grandsons thinking they want to be like you and start skipping school like you." She moved in again. "Bend down so I can tell you something else."

I obeyed and bent down so my ear was near her head. She whispered. "If you ever skip school again, I will personally come over and drag you back to school." Then she kissed my cheek.

I felt something well up inside of me and nodded my thanks as I quickly moved away. I could hardly see as tears threatened to start pouring down my face. By the time I reached my house, I was a mess. I had managed not to feel anything for days. The voice inside my head told me I was so weak. How could I let an old lady melt me into a big baby? I had managed to go over and over in my head that Hancock would be better without me. I should have kept walking when I saw Mrs. Wilkes. Why did she have to say those things to me? Why did she make me think I mattered? Guilt came screaming back.

I found myself inside my house, alone. I swung myself into my room and opened my sock drawer to grab the pill bottle and threw it on my bed. Then I tossed my crutches onto the floor as I fell down on my bed and cried. Cried like the big baby I was. I was thankful I was alone. What would Mom, Dad, or even Vic say if they saw me crying like a baby? This was not the strong pro football player they were all raising. I was such a failure. I didn't deserve to live. But I had lost the numb feeling. I was no longer in control.

It was only 10 am and I was falling apart. I grabbed the pill bottle, but couldn't open the lid. I forced it so hard that when it finally came off the pills flew all over the room. I cursed and picked up the one closest to me. My tears made it hard to see the others scattered all over my floor. I tried to bend down and crawl on the floor to find the others, but my knee was killing me. It was over. My plan had failed.

I looked down into my palm and there was the one small pill I had picked up. One. I popped it in my mouth and swallowed. I knew it would only do the one thing it needed to do. Help the growing pain in my knee. Then I crawled back onto my bed and cried until I fell asleep.

Chapter 35

Help

I wasn't sure what time it was when I heard pounding on my door. For a minute, I couldn't remember where I was. It was that very long minute that caused whoever was at the door to open it on their own.

"OZZIE? CAN YOU HEAR ME? POLICE OFFICER EVANS HERE! OZZIE?" The voice boomed through the house.

"IN HERE!" I responded. My heart began to beat quickly. I wondered what time it was, so I glanced at my phone and saw it was 3:30. I'd slept most of the day. What was wrong that the police were coming into my house? Was one of my parents in a car accident? Or Vic? I sat up quickly, but pain shot through my knee, reminding me I couldn't stand up on my own yet. So I stayed seated on the edge of my bed.

A very skinny white cop, about Dad's age, peaked around the corner into my room. His eyes searched my hands and he scanned the room as he slowly moved into my doorway. "Ozzie, are you alone?" He asked as his eyes continued to assess me.

I could see him relax a little as I nodded. "Yes, sir. Is everything okay? Are my parents alright?"

Officer Evans nodded to someone in the hall who then showed herself. The black officer was twice Evan's size. "This is Officer Grace." She nodded at me as she scanned the room, taking over for Officer Evans. This let him move in closer to me. "Ozzie, I'm sure your parents are fine. But we are here because we received a call about you. There was reason to believe that you were trying to kill yourself.

I was surprised and confused. I didn't know what to say. "I didn't try to kill myself." I joked awkwardly. "I'm not dead, am I?"

Officer Evans spoke into his police radio. "We are 10–4. Roll EMS." He then smiled at me. "That may be, Ozzie, but I've just asked EMS, who have been on standby down the street, to come on in. They will check you out and make sure you *are* okay."

"But I *am* okay." I argued. But I wasn't okay, and I knew it. I had been too weak to follow through with my plan.

Officer Grace moved in behind me and reached for my covers. She lifted them and found the empty pain pill bottle. She grabbed it and handed them to Officer Evans. "Did you take all of these?" He asked.

I shook my head. "No, sir." I glanced at the floor. "Only one for my pain." Officer Grace was already picking up the scattered pills. She handed Officer Evans the loose pills and he shoved them back into the bottle.

He looked at the bottle carefully and then counted the ones they had gathered. "Ozzie, the bottle says it had 30 pills, but there are only 10 left."

I shook my head and pointed at my leg. "I tore my ACL over three weeks ago. I took those other ones early on."

"But there are 10 left," he stated.

"So?" I was not very happy. I wouldn't be having this conversation if I had taken all of them.

"Were you saving these?" He asked.

I didn't answer. At that moment I heard the front door open and close again. EMS had arrived. A large Hispanic woman walked through my bedroom door followed by two more paramedics, both young white men. Their wide eyes told me they were new. They seemed relieved to find me still alive. The smallest trainee hauled in a huge box and opened it immediately as the female paramedic talked to me. "Your name is Ozzie, right?" Officer Evans showed her my pain pills and she nodded. She now knew what she was looking for.

"Yes, ma'am," I said as she looked carefully at my pupils. She listened to my chest and took my pulse before she took a deep breath. She was happy with what she found.

"Can you tell me how you are feeling?" She pulled out a blood pressure cuff as she waited for me to respond.

"I'm fine." I was not sure how to respond, really. "Well, my leg still hurts, but I'm sure that's not why you're here."

"Can you tell me why I *am* here, Ozzie?" She smiled and finished taking my blood pressure, nodding at her team. My pressure must have been good. She slid a little plastic clip onto my finger as she asked again, "Ozzie, tell me what is going on?" The plastic finger clip blinked and she said out loud, "Your oxygen looks good too."

"So nothing is wrong. Right?" I was slipping into a fog. Too much was happening too fast, and none of it felt real.

The paramedic nodded to Officer Evans who walked up to me as the paramedics began packing up their equipment. She smiled at me again, "Maybe you would like to speak with Officer Evans." She patted my hand. "I know this has been a lot, but you need to talk about it. My team and I will be waiting in the other room." I nodded but was not sure I understood why I should care where she was.

Officer Evans pulled up my desk chair and sat in front of me. "Ozzie, are you thinking about killing yourself?"

I looked to my open door where Officer Grace stood looking down the hall as if she was not paying attention. But I knew she was listening to every word. There were too many strangers. Why should strangers care if no one else cared about me?

"Ozzie, are you going to kill yourself?" He asked a little more firmly. "We are really worried about you and so are your friends.

I frowned. "My friends?"

"Are you strong enough to stand up?" He asked me. I nodded. So he handed me the crutches that I had thrown further away from my bed than I remembered. We walked over to my window and he pointed at three figures standing in the driveway. Zonta, Lilly, and Vashon were leaning into each other. Vashon had his long skinny arms wrapped around both girls' shoulders. At another time and place I would have smiled, but that afternoon I couldn't.

"Did they call you?" I asked as I swung myself back over to sit on the bed.

"They did." He settled himself back in the chair.

"How did they know?" I was confused. I went over and over in my head how I had given away my plans.

"They will have to tell you that." He paused and then added, "So, you *are* planning on killing yourself?" I had just confessed. He was good. Very good. I finally nodded. Something began to unravel inside me. I tried to push it down again. To save that guilt and self-hate for another day. For next time. But the officer wasn't finished. "Do you have a plan?"

The unraveling took over again. The numbness had faded and the guilt returned. I couldn't control the guilt. I couldn't control my self-hate. I couldn't lie to this kind man, who owed me nothing. So I didn't hesitate to look at the bottle Officer Evans was still holding. I had failed. Again.

Officer Evans saw the disappointment in my eyes as he looked at the pills. "Well, it is a good thing you didn't."

"Is it?" I asked.

"Tell me why you ask that?" Officer Evans shoved the pills into his coat pocket.

I didn't want to, but I couldn't help spilling my secrets to this stranger. "I don't think I'm much good to anyone. I screw up everyone's life."

"If that were the case you wouldn't have three friends out there worrying about you." He was very calm and factual. He didn't make me feel like I was stupid for even trying. "Do you want to talk to them?" I felt something break loose again. This time, I felt tears well up, but I still nodded. Officer Evans pulled out his radio and told some officer outside to bring in my friends. *Friends*. Strange word. Officer

Evans turned and looked at me again. "Ozzie, we will let you talk to them a few minutes, but then EMS will transport you to the hospital."

"Why?" Panic set in. I knew Dad and Mom would be upset.

"It's procedure. We need doctors to evaluate you and make sure you won't hurt yourself." His smile was gentle. I stared at him, shocked. All of my screwups ran through my head. And this was the biggest screwup of all. Everything would get worse. The officer walked back over to me and squatted down to look straight at me. "Ozzie. This is a good thing. You are a normal person going through a really bad time." I shook my head trying to hold off his words. I was not normal. I was messed up. But he continued, "I've been where you are now. Believe me, a lot of people have. All of us for different reasons. Sometimes reasons no one else can understand." I looked at the officer. He wasn't messing with me to get his way. He was real. I kept eye contact as he added, "But the truth is you don't EVER have to go through this again. You are not alone." Suddenly I felt the rest of me break loose. And I started crying. Again. Officer Evans embraced me as I leaned into his shoulders. My huge size felt like it was collapsing on him, so Officer Grace came in to help him hold me up. They both held onto me. They didn't tell me to shut up. They didn't tell me I was a loser. Or weak. Officer Evans was not finished. "You are showing strength right now. To be a man worth anything you have to be able to let go and not give a damn about who you *think* you should be. You have to look forward to who you can become." For the first time in years, I felt lighter. Officer Evans had begun to chip away at something I didn't know I could let go.

Chapter 36

Friends

As soon as I pulled away from the two officers, I looked up to find three new people standing in the room staring at me. My friends. Vashon was wide-eyed and sweating. "Man! You scared me!"

Officer Evans pulled away and nodded at Officer Grace to follow him. "We will give you a few minutes and wait for you in the hall." He took my phone and asked to get my dad's number. I unlocked the screen and handed it to him. He walked out the door leaving the four of us alone.

Lilly plopped down on the bed next to me. "Are you okay?" Zonta stood quietly at the door taking it all in. Her face was tear-streaked. Like mine.

I looked at Lilly. "I'm okay." There was silence. I knew that they had no idea what to say, so I asked, "How did you know?"

Lilly pulled my folded letter out of her pocket and waved it at me. "You sent Zonta and me a goodbye note."

"It wasn't a goodbye note," I argued.

"Yes, it was!" She held up the letter. "*Dear Lilly, sorry for everything I've done. I hope you have a great life and hope one day you will forgive me. Ozzie.*" She waved the letter at me. "You basically said *have a nice life.* Since I wasn't going anywhere, I knew something was up. But Zonta didn't give me the letter until after school. That's when I read it."

"I didn't see them until the end of the day." Zonta was defensive.

"It's not your fault, Zonta," Lilly stated. "He didn't want us to find them earlier."

"That's when they found me." Vashon was itching to tell his side of the story. He reached into his backpack and pulled out my Browns cap. "I saw Blake in the hall. Never spoken to him before, but I asked him why he had your cap and he told me you'd given it to him. I knew then you were sick in the head. You've never let anyone else wear that." He held the cap gently and looked at it. "I would know since I've been trying for years. So I grabbed it off Blake's head and ran." I smiled at Vashon as he handed me the soft brown cap. I took it and let my fingers run over the stitching. The orange and white letters stood out like old friends. Vashon wasn't finished. "I found the girls in the hall and they told me something was wrong, which I knew. We all decided we should call 911."

"So then Vashon called 911 and told them what we thought." Lilly continued. "After that Zonta drove us here in her sweet ride."

My leg felt stiff as I tried to move. "I don't know what to say." How could I ever express how much this meant to me.

"You can say you'll not kill yourself." Lilly was straightforward.

"Well, I didn't! Did I?" I argued. But a warmth spread through me. I could feel myself smile. Just a little.

"No, you didn't." She looked at me. "What stopped you?"

"I messed up," I said, remembering my walk down Hall Drive.

"Messed up?" Vashon asked.

I took a deep breath. Thankful for the first time that I was still breathing. "I talked to your granny." My smile grew.

Vashon smiled. "Oh, man! That will do it."

"What do you mean?" Zonta asked, still holding her distance.

I saw Vashon begin to speak, but he stopped and waited for me to explain. So I did. "Mrs. Wilkes always makes us remember what it means to be from Hall. She reminds us that we are a community and that we look out for each other. And that, somehow, I am a piece of a puzzle here that matters."

Vashon's eyes got really big. "She said all that? I thought you were going to say that she'd whoop you if you did anything stupid."

I smiled. "Well, yeah, that too!"

We all laughed. Even Zonta.

Chapter 37

The Plan

Ten minutes later, EMS took me to the hospital to begin the process of evaluating my safety. Officer Evans said he'd check on me the next day. I believed him.

Dad and Vic were at the hospital by the time I arrived. They didn't say much. But the look of fear on their faces said enough. Mom left whatever large-scale event she had planned in Chicago and drove nonstop to finally walk into my hospital room by midnight. I kept telling everyone I was fine. But I knew I wasn't. The docs and my parents agreed to check me into the psych unit for observation and to make sure we had a plan.

"What plan?" Vic asked, two days later, as Mom and Dad sat in a small conference room with the doctor sitting next to me. My family was not allowed into the psych unit with me, but everyone could meet with me in one of the side rooms.

The doctor was quick to explain. "It will need to be a plan to make sure Ozzie does not go down this dark path again."

Mom was not even trying to hide that she was crying. I don't think she had stopped crying for the last two days. "Whatever we need to do, Doctor."

Dad reached over to grab Mom's hand and squeeze it.

"I am sorry, Doctor." Vic kept shifting in his chair. "I'm trying to understand this. But it makes no sense!"

I felt myself take a deep breath, just like the therapists had taught me. I needed to be ready to talk about it. I wasn't sure I was. But Vic's words began to stir that old voice deep inside me.

"Please explain what you mean, Vic?" The doctor said softly.

Vic looked at me when he answered. "You have everything! You have a great home with parents who love you. Pay attention here, Ozzie! You have a mother *and* a father! Everyone looks up to you. You are practically a superstar. You have the best chance to play for the NFL one day." Vic threw up his arms. "Why would you even throw it all away because you have a stupid torn ACL? Or because you broke up with some slutty girl?"

"Don't you talk about Zonta that way." I felt the guilt return, but this time I didn't push it down, I let it pour out of me. "Only reason everyone thinks she is slutty is because I didn't stop a horrible rumor.

I let her suffer because I wasn't man enough to shut up the rumors!" I felt tears flow again, but I didn't care. "If you think I wanted to die because I tore my ACL, then you are really blind. All this is your dream. Not mine. I tried. I swear I tried to love it like you and Dad. And there are a few days I have. But mostly, I push through and make myself and everyone else believe I love it." I swallowed but quickly went on. "But I am done pretending. I can't live your dream, Vic." I looked at Dad. "Or yours, Dad." Dad just nodded as tears fell.

"Wait just a second, Ozzie!" Vic argued. "You always made us believe you wanted it. Even when I called you out and asked if you even cared, you pushed back." Vic shook his head as he stared right at me. "We never meant . . ."

"I'm not done." I stopped him. Vic was right, I never had let them know. Why hadn't I told them earlier? None of this would be happening if I had just told them earlier. I felt the old guilt seep back, but instead of tucking it away, I spoke. "I know you never meant to. And I *should* have said something. But I didn't. All I ever wanted was to please you and make you both proud of me. The only way I knew how was to be the best lineman." There was silence. "And I was."

It was a full thirty seconds before Vic answered. "Yes, you were."

Dad whispered, "You still are."

"But that is not who I really am," I said. Suddenly, I felt something inside me loosen. "I don't know who I really am."

"You're a Waxman." Mom smiled through her tears. "And we are fighters."

Vic leaned back in his chair. "That's for sure."

"Ozzie, do you want to say anything else before you return to your room?" The doctor asked.

"Yes," I looked at Mom, at Dad, and then let my eyes rest on Vic, who was still staring at me. Like he was trying to understand me for the first time. "I need you all to help me figure this out. Whatever the *this* in my life is going to be."

That day we developed a plan. The keyword was *we*. Mom and Dad agreed to do family counseling if I agreed to continue therapy on my own for at least a year. I said I would.

Vic said he'd do his part too, and he and I both knew that meant he would need to be a part of working through my issues. I was surprised he wasn't angry. He seemed relieved. A part of me thought it was strange. I thought he would think it weak or lame to *deal with your feelings*. But the truth was, the relief in Vic's eyes showed me he was thankful I gave him the excuse to deal with those "feelings." As brothers, we grew up learning to be the toughest, baddest football players in Hancock. It seemed we needed to relearn how to be brothers.

The plan also included surgery, postponed a month to make sure I was ready. Then rehab for my knee to build back its strength. Then, and only then, would I decide if I would play football again. Everyone agreed it would be my decision. Mine alone.

Hancock High won the championship without me. But I was okay.

I had a lot of time to think. I could still see Zonta keeping her distance from me, leaning against my bedroom door. She had worried about me enough to help Lilly and Vashon call 911 and then drove them to my house to find me. But even in her worry for me, she didn't trust me. I decided to do what I should have done a long time ago. I took out my phone and posted that Zonta and I had *not* hooked up and made sure everyone knew that it was a stupid rumor. A rumor that I had never tried to stop. I hoped the post would help her forgive me, but I knew it would take time.

I had a long way to go. But I suddenly felt like going there. I suddenly cared.

Chapter 38

Think about it?

"Did you ever think about it?" I asked Lilly. School had just let out for winter break. I was actually putting weight on my right leg as I walked with her to the bus stop. I missed the support the crutches offered me, but I was making good progress. A custom-made, knee brace gave me the confidence I needed. Enough confidence that I had decided to do surgery in January. I was actually looking forward to it.

Snow was coming down, and a small dusting of white powder was covering the road. County trucks had already prepped the roads with a layer of salt and dirt. So the thin layer of white disappeared as soon as it formed. My Browns cap helped keep the snow from hitting my face, but my ears were freezing. Lilly moved slowly next to me, letting me walk at my own pace. "Think about what?" She asked looking at me. A few strands of recently cut *and* highlighted hair poked out from under her red wool cap and her nose was turning pink. I was happy to see she was wearing a warm blue jacket and avoided asking where she got it. I didn't know how long she would live with Zonta, but I thought, maybe, that Lilly was happier.

I felt my cheeks warm and I looked away. We settled onto the bench at the bus stop together after Lilly wiped off the thin layer of snow. She was waiting for me to answer. I saw we were alone, so I finally dared. "You know? Kill yourself?" It felt like I was pushing it. What made me think I could ask anyone that question? I quickly tried to take it back. "Never mind. Stupid question."

I could feel Lilly staring at me and she didn't say anything until I finally looked at her. I wondered if I would ever get used to her green eyes. I stared a little too long, but I didn't look away as she smiled. Just a small, knowing smile. "Maybe." She squinted at the bus stop sign like she was trying to look at something in particular. Her eyes went wide and one finger shot into the air. "There was that one time . . ."

"I told you never mind!" I stopped her before she went on. Then I pretended to look down the road to see if the bus was coming. It wasn't.

She slapped my shoulder. "Don't interrupt me when I'm sharing!" I rolled my eyes at her. She slapped me again, a little harder. "Seriously! Listen."

So I leaned back against the bench and folded my arms across my chest. "Alright, go on."

Lilly pulled her old backpack onto her lap and pointed at a small blue ribbon she had tied to the bottom of one strap. "This ribbon reminds me every day why I am alive." She gently touched the very dirty piece of fabric. "When I was little, my granny used to braid my hair and tie the ends with blue ribbon. She would make me stand in front of her so she could look at me. All of me. And then she would smile and tell me I was the most beautiful blond she'd ever seen and that the blue made my magic shine." Lilly didn't take her eyes off the ribbon. "So I believed her. I felt pretty, at first. But it was more than that. I felt strong . . . bulletproof." She looked at me and smiled like a young child. "It really felt like magic." Her smile faded as she continued. "Then, when I started school, I realized that I wasn't pretty. Not the way the other girls are pretty. I wasn't even blond . . . just dirty blond." Lilly quickly swallowed and let go of the ribbon in order to touch the blond-highlighted strand of hair poking out from under her cap. A cool breeze hit us in the face, so she zipped her blue jacket up to her chin. "But Granny told me that it didn't matter, the magic was still there. And only some could see it." Lilly looked straight at me and smirked as she added, "And she said anyone who couldn't see it could go to hell!" The shock on my face made Lilly laugh.

"Well, I don't think I'd like to meet her anytime soon. She'd probably whoop me." I smiled.

"She's dead. Cancer killed her when I was fourteen." Lilly looked at the bus stop sign again.

"Oh. I didn't know. Sorry." I looked down the street again.

She didn't say anything for a few minutes and then looked at me again. "You see, Granny told me that nobody owes me anything and I don't owe anybody anything. I can make my own magic. Or not." Lilly looked away and then I saw her eyes begin to water. I had never seen Lilly cry, really cry and not try to push it away. Never thought she knew how to cry. "I wanted to die with Granny the night she died. She was my whole world. She was the only one who believed in me. I told Granny I wanted to die and go with her. But she squeezed my hand and made me look right at her." Lilly looked at me and she let the tears fall without wiping them. She was still fearless. "She told me that if I died with her then I would be killing her all over again. That everything she had taught me, every bit of the magic she had poured into me, would die too. And that if I died, then she could no longer be in my life, so as long as I lived, she would be right here with me."

I felt my throat tighten and I sniffed back my own tears. "She's your history."

Lilly looked at me. "What?"

I smiled and explained, "She was what you were talking about the first day you walked into history class. She is the history that tells you who you are today."

Lilly nodded and smiled back at me. "I knew you were different that first day of school. You were just too stubborn to show it or even know it."

Bus 66 surprised us as it pulled up. This time we both got on. Zonta had left school early and said we were to all come to a Christmas party at her house. Zonta was still not sure of me, but she was letting me back into her circle. That was good enough for me. Lilly and I settled into the back of the bus before I dared to speak. I whispered. "Thanks, Lilly."

She snorted, "For what?" She wiped her face on her sleeve.

"For sharing Granny with me." I looked at the blue ribbon. "And your magic."

Lilly laughed out loud and slapped my shoulder again. "I swear if you tell anyone, I *will* kill you!"

I laughed. Really laughed. It had been a long time.

Ozzie

Acknowledgements

Writing Ozzie could never have happened without the help of several individuals. A special thanks to all of the following people who played a role in the process. I am forever grateful to each of you for the time and support you provided. Your engagement in the story and responses to the characters inspire me to continue on this journey into the world of Hancock High.

To my parents Jonlyn and G. Keith Parker, who were willing to take on the first read-through of the manuscript *and* multiple additional drafts. They have not only embraced the characters' lives with gusto, but they have shown unwavering support for the whole writing process. To Ben Onachila, who also was willing to take on the first read-through and provide me with refreshing feedback. His uncanny poetic ability has helped me iron out some rough edges. To my daughters, Maya Borhaug and Sarah Borhaug, whose read-throughs helped me keep the story and characters real. To Kym Sebranek, Sheila Mooney, Jennifer Sensabaugh, Jose Rene Perez, Michael Bower, Mary Ann Galyon and Dr. Tara P. Bacote for reading through the manuscript and providing valuable feedback, each bringing their unique perspective to the table, supporting my desire to provide an authentic story. To Nastia Parker for not only reading through the manuscript but guiding me through the intricate world of social media and texting trends.

Brevard North Carolina's former Police Chief, Phil Harris, for details on police procedure and terminology and Dan Essenberg for educating me on the ins and outs of High School football and its ever-changing canvas.

Lashunn Dialo Gardin (Harper) for his willingness to model for the cover and read through the manuscript. My daughter, Amy Borhaug, who whispers words of perseverance and courage. Nioca Robinson, whose encouragement I dearly value.

My copy editor Julie Overpeck, who not only understands the importance of Hi-Lo books, but helped turn out a professional product.

A special thanks to Transylvania County Schools and Brevard High School for the use of their property for the cover shot.

Sarah Borhaug's time, commitment, creativity and professional skill in shooting, editing and designing the cover are deeply appreciated.

Last but not least, my husband, Tore, for his unwavering support and his steady grounding. Without him, none of it would be possible.

Ozzie's Text/Slang/Terms

The following are definitions of terms, including texting and slang, used in *Ozzie*. Some terms may also have other definitions that are not included in this mini-glossary.

2—to, too, two

8—ate

bite guard— a piece of plastic that fits into the mouth to protect the teeth and tongue

defense— in football, when the team does not have ball tries to keep the other team from scoring

dis— insult/offend

end zone— in football, area on field where team scores points

gn—goodnight

k—okay

line of scrimmage— in football, the area on the field where each play begins

offense— in football, when the team has the ball and is trying to score

omg—oh my gosh/God/goodness

pic—picture

plays— in football, the action plan that is to be used to move the ball down the field

quarterback— in football, a player on offense that calls plays and will throw the ball, hand the ball off, or run with the ball

r—are

ride shotgun— ride in the front seat next to the driver

running back— in football, on offense this player is one who often carries the ball in an attempt to score

shook—surprised/shocked

tackle— Verb: in football, to take the person with the ball to the ground. Noun: a player that is usually biggest and strongest on team. The player either blocks others from getting to key players (offense), or rushes players/stops players on other team from scoring (defense)

thanx—thanks

touchdown—in football, to score six points by taking the football into the opponents end zone

u—you

ur—you're/your

we are 10-4— situation is stable/okay

whack—messed up

winging it— making it up as you go

wyd—what are you doing?